A MEMORY
Like You

VICKIE FISHER

Year of the Book
135 Glen Avenue
Glen Rock, PA 17327

Print ISBN: 978-1-64649-126-1
Ebook ISBN: 978-1-64649-127-8

Cover design by PixelStudio

This book is a work of fiction. All characters except for the spiritual hero are fictitious. If you happen to see your name, then thank you for having such an awesome name. I just had to use it, but the character is a figment of my imagination.

Scripture verses are taken from the King James, New International, and English Standard Versions of the Bible.

To learn more about the author check out her website at: vickiefisher.com.

Dedication

To every woman who has ever had a dream.
I hope it comes true.

Acknowledgments

First and foremost I have to acknowledge God for creating within me the love of writing. For Your son Jesus, without Him nothing would be worthwhile.

It takes a village to move a book to the finish line and into readers hands. I love my village—you are the best. To my editor and publisher, Demi Stevens and Year of the Book, you are awesome. To my posse who makes it look like I know what I am doing, what would I do without you?

A special thanks to Google, YouTube, and the Cowboy Channel—you made researching this book fun.

Thanks also to Justin Stonestreet for answering my questions about bull riding.

Chapter 1

"Little early to be heading over to the school, isn't it?" Hank McDaniel asked his daughter Cassidy as she put the saddle on her mare, Cleopatra.

"It's a beautiful day, thought we would ride out and check the fences along the road."

Hank took his hat off and wiped the sweat from his forehead with his sleeve. "Too hot for fence work."

"I didn't say I was fixing them." She laughed. "I'm just looking to see if they need you and Jake to fix them."

"Funny girl." He flicked her black cowgirl hat off her head.

"Hey." She caught it as it fell past her face. Putting it back on, she said, "We'll stop at the stream to cool off with a good drink of spring water." Cleopatra neighed and nodded her head.

Hank chuckled. "Sometimes I think that horse is actually talking to you."

Cassidy stroked Cleopatra's neck. "She is."

Hank laid his hand on the horse's hindquarters. "She's one of a kind."

"One of a pair," Cassidy corrected and put her finger to her lips. "But it's best not to say his name."

"Sure would like to know where they came from." Hank followed Cassidy and her horse out of the barn and opened the paddock gate.

"The story I tell is they were born of the lake." Cassidy sprang up into the saddle.

Hank grinned. "Then you should have named her Lady and someone else Arthur."

Stroking her horse's neck, she said, "Lady would have been nice, but Cleopatra is perfect."

Hank rubbed the neck of the pure black quarter horse. "You are a beauty. If you had papers you could finally be the horse of the year."

"It might not be official, but everyone knows they are the best two horses on the circuit."

"That they are."

Shane grimaced when the sign for Yellowstone came into view, and waited for the words he knew were coming from his girlfriend, Jennifer.

"Are we there yet?"

"Have I stopped driving yet?"

She slapped his arm. "Shane Cartwright, there's no need to be so cantankerous."

"It's not like you haven't asked the same question a thousand times."

She folded her arms across her chest. "Well, how much longer?"

"Sign said Yellowstone, hundred miles."

"A hundred miles?" she whined.

"How many times do I have to tell you we aren't going to Yellowstone? We're going thirty miles north of Cody. So settle down, we still have a while."

"I didn't realize your parents were so far away."

"I told you eight hours. Add hauling a horse trailer, and it becomes ten. Then add in all the stops you need to make and..." He squeezed her hand. "You get the point."

"I thought you were joking."

"I wasn't."

"I see that now." She grabbed the magazine that had fallen to the floor and flipped its pages. Ten miles down the road another sign for Yellowstone loomed ahead. As if on cue, she said, "Are we there yet?"

"If you ask one more time, I am going to pull over and wait until you grow some patience." The minute the words were out of his mouth he started to laugh.

She hit him with her magazine. "What is so funny?"

"I've turned into my father." He wiped the tears from his eyes. "He used to say that very thing when we were kids."

"Did he pull over?"

"No, my mother wouldn't allow it." He grinned. "But she isn't here, so don't tempt your luck."

"You are so ill-mannered." She glared at him. "What I see in you is beyond me." He couldn't stop laughing.

Jennifer huffed and ripped open her magazine. An hour later they passed the exit sign off the highway for Yellowstone. He could feel her squirming in her seat. This time she held her tongue. He stared at the road ahead. Forty-five minutes from now he would be home for the first time in five years.

Taking the exit, a wave of dread filled his gut. For a moment he wondered if it was too late to turn back. After all, no one knew they were coming. He felt the burger he had eaten hours ago turn to lead as he passed the sign welcoming him into his hometown of Berksville, Wyoming. Five years and Main Street hadn't changed a bit. The Grand Hotel stood in all her former glory, greeting visitors as they entered the city limits. Besides, it was the best place to eat in town. The Cattleman's Diner. Other than the pizza shop, one street over, it was the only place to eat. He smiled to himself. That was where he'd taken Cassidy on their first date. He felt a jolt to his heart as he always did when her name crossed his mind.

"Is that where the rodeo is?" Jennifer asked.

Shane didn't have to glance to his right to know she had pointed at the biggest and newest place in town... the Berksville Arena. Behind the domed arena was the livestock auction. It was where he had first held—*Stop! This is not a drive down memory lane. Get it together.*

"Looks small."

"It's not."

Sam and Clyde sat in wicker rocking chairs in front of the feed store, probably telling the same stories he had heard as a kid. He waved at them and watched in amusement as their jaws flew open when they recognized him. Clyde stood up. He could almost hear him say, "Hey, isn't that the Cartwright kid?"

Halfway down the block Shane almost slammed on his brakes. "Man! What happened to the bank?" He stared at the boarded up plate glass window.

"You think someone tried to rob it?"

"That would be a shocker." Shane shook his head. "There's never been any crime here."

"What is this, Mayberry?" He didn't have to see it to know she had rolled her eyes. "No wonder you left this town and never looked back."

"Because there's no crime?"

"You know that is not what I meant." She wildly waved her hand. "Look at this place. It's like time forgot it existed. I would have hightailed it out of here the second I could have, too."

"It was a great place to grow up."

"That's why you left."

"The town isn't the reason I left."

"I know." She patted his leg. "You like Colorado and its nightlife better."

If only that were true.

Jennifer pointed to his left. "I think that woman is waving at us."

Shane slowed the truck to a crawl and rolled down his window. "Hey, Mrs. Jenkins. Nice to see you." He watched her in his rearview mirror pull out her cellphone. "Well, there goes the surprise. Within minutes the whole town will know I'm home."

"I don't understand why you didn't even call your parents and let them know we were coming."

"I told you, I wanted to surprise them."

"But why?"

5

He shrugged his shoulders. At the time, it had made sense. If he didn't tell anyone they were coming, they couldn't tell Cassidy. And she couldn't withdraw from this weekend's rodeo. Because he knew without a doubt if he was going to be there, she wouldn't be.

He glanced at Jennifer. For a moment he wondered if Cassidy would even care he had brought home a woman. Nah, after all this time, she probably had someone of her own. A sharp pain pierced his heart. No one had ever mentioned if she dated anyone. *What does it matter?* His hands tightened around the steering wheel until they were almost white. He took a deep breath trying to force himself to relax. He rubbed his forehead.

Coming home was a mistake. Every inch of this town held memories of her. Who was he kidding? It wasn't just this place. He had avoided the whole state of Wyoming for the last five years because of her. Today the memories had started when they crossed from Colorado into Wyoming, mile by mile forming until they became a tornado whirling inside of him. Why had he thought he could do this?

"How much longer?"

He bit his tongue. It wasn't Jennifer's fault he was dying inside. He reached across the seat for her hand. Cassidy had been pretty, but Jennifer was Hollywood glamorous. He squeezed her hand gently. "About twenty miles."

Jennifer dug in her purse for her lipstick. He watched as she opened the mirror on the visor and took a moment to admire herself before fluffing her long blonde hair and applying red lipstick.

Cassidy would never—*stop it.* He gripped the steering wheel. Cassidy McDaniel was history. So why did the sight of the wooden fence of the McDaniel's ranch have his lunch turn to bile in his stomach? It took all he had not to turn and look down their driveway. This was definitely a bad idea.

A few miles down the road, he could see a lone rider on horseback. His heart filled with a warm glow that spread through his whole body. Cassidy. He would know her anywhere, even from a mile away. If the long black braid swinging with the motion of the beautiful black horse wasn't enough, the black hat with the flowery pink scarf tied around the brim screamed Cassidy. His heart pounded so loud he wondered how Jennifer couldn't hear it. Five years and he still felt the pull of the only woman he had ever loved.

Antony started whinnying and stomping his hoofs. "What is wrong with your horse?" Jennifer asked.

"What?"

"You don't hear him making all that racket?"

"Probably knows he'll be home soon."

She waved her hand around. "This isn't home." Jennifer leaned over and kissed him on the mouth. "Home is with me in Colorado."

Shane pushed her away. "What did you do that for? I'm trying to drive here."

Cassidy rode the wooden fence line along the main road, talking to Cleopatra. "What a beautiful day to be checking for broken fences. The sun's shining, there's a gentle breeze, the birds are singing and not a trouble in sight." She could see the corner where McDaniel land met the Cartwrights. Her heart quivered, followed by tiny butterflies fluttering inside her. She put a hand on her stomach. What was wrong with her? The sight of the Cartwrights' land didn't affect her.

Cleo took a stutter step. "What's wrong girl?" The mare turned her head and gave a loud neigh.

Cassidy slowly turned in the saddle and looked at the black truck pulling a sleek black and silver horse trailer heading toward her. It was too far away to see the driver, but she knew. The pull of her heart told her Shane had come home.

In horror, she watched blonde hair block his face from view. Cassidy's blood froze. She couldn't breathe. He'd brought someone home with him. Not just anyone, her heart screamed, a blonde someone. Was it Miranda?

Cassidy spun Cleopatra around and squeezed her legs into the horse's sides, forcing her to gallop. The mare turned her head to look at the truck. "Yeah girl, you feel him too, don't you?" Cassidy put a little more pressure until they were galloping at full speed. She had to get away from there before he saw her.

His heart threatened to squeeze the life out of him as he watched Cassidy fly across the field. He fought the urge to stop the truck and run after her. Seeing her even from a distance had flipped his insides worse than any bull could have done. And in that instant, he knew his mother had been right. There was a difference between love and lust. Love was pulling his heart right out of his chest and bolting across the land, while lust burned a whole lot less than it had ten hours ago.

Jennifer was pulling on his arm. "What is wrong with you?"

"What?"

"How can you keep ignoring your horse trying to break down the trailer?"

Shane glanced back behind the truck. "He'll calm himself down in a minute. He just senses Cleopatra." Shane watched as Cassidy and the mare disappeared over the hill. How many times had he made her mad and she took off riding like that to get away from him? Only to have him catch up to her at the shade tree by the stream, where they would kiss and make up.

"Cleopatra?"

"Cassidy's horse."

"Cleopatra and Antony." Jennifer glared back at the trailer. "How cute."

"We were kids when we named them."

Jennifer bit her lip. "Why would Antony think her horse was near?"

Shane pointed to the green pasture to his left. "This is the McDaniel ranch."

Jennifer frowned. "I didn't realize their property was this close to yours."

"Neighbors."

"Humph." Her frown deepened. "So the 'girl next door' was really the girl next door."

"If you consider ten miles next door. Five, if you cut through the meadows."

Jennifer rolled her eyes. "I'm sure you did that more than once." The sign for C&M Rodeo School came into view. "Is that your family's school?"

"Yes."

She stared at him for a long moment. "Let me guess. The M is for McDaniel."

"Sure is."

"You just couldn't get away from her, could you?" She touched up the red lipstick once again. "Lucky for me you've outgrown boring."

"Lucky." Why didn't he feel lucky? A few minutes down the road, he turned into the two-mile-long driveway of the family ranch. No matter what Jennifer thought, this would always be home. The tall iron Double C sign over the driveway did not bring with it the sense of belonging it always had. Instead, regret washed over him. This was not his home. He had run away from it five years ago. He glanced across the land he loved. Somewhere over the hills and down in the valley was the reason he had left.

Jennifer gasped as they crested the hill and the house came into sight. "You didn't tell me it was so beautiful."

Shane looked at the property as if for the first time. The large two-story white farmhouse stood out against the rustic landscape like a belle at the ball. The way the sun cast parts in shadows gave it an air of mystery. And yet the wraparound porch with hanging flower baskets and roses lining the sidewalk gave it that welcoming touch. A hint of the red barn could be seen peeping around the corner.

The front door flew open and his mother came running out. For the first time since he had started this journey home, Shane felt good about it.

There was nothing he would like more than to be wrapped in his mother's arms, but he had a horse to calm down. He waved and kept driving to the barn.

"We aren't stopping at the house first?"

"Not with a horse about to tear down my trailer."

"Now you care." She grabbed his arm. "Stop. I have to use the bathroom."

"It's just a short walk from the barn to the house. You can hold it." He pulled up in front of the barn, opened the truck door, and started to get out, then glanced over at Jennifer. "Oh, I forgot to mention two house rules. We won't be sharing a room and there is no alcohol allowed."

"What?" She threw her magazine, hitting him in the face. "You tell me this now?" Jennifer glared at him.

He jumped down from the truck and slammed the door behind him. Opening the side door to the trailer, he stepped in and patted Antony's neck. "You couldn't see her, but you knew she was there, didn't you?"

His father, Jason, stuck his head in the doorway. "What's got him all hyped up?"

Shane continued to stroke his stallion's neck. "Somehow he knew a certain lady horse was nearby."

The last thing he needed to do was say the name aloud. There would be no calming him down then.

His father stepped up into the trailer with a laugh. "Wow. After all these years, he still remembers her."

"True love."

"Love is a strange thing." Jason patted his son on the back. "Animal or human doesn't make much difference. When it's real, there is no running from it. I'm assuming she wasn't out there by herself."

Shane shook his head.

"Did you talk to her?"

"Of course not."

His mother Ann squeezed into the trailer. "Antony, calm yourself down. I haven't seen my boy since the last rodeo a month ago. This is my time." Surprisingly, Antony stopped snorting and prancing. Ann kissed the horse on the nose. "That's a good boy."

Jason laughed and backed out of the small space. "Your mom, the horse whisperer."

Shane picked his mother up into a bear hug. He kissed her cheek. "Missed you, Mom."

She laughed. "Put me down." When her feet hit the ground, she stepped out of the trailer, followed by Shane. "Tell me why I had to hear from Mable Jenkins you were in town?"

"Wanted it to be a surprise."

"That it is." She hugged him again. "Words cannot express how glad it makes my heart feel to have you home. It's been too long."

Chapter 2

At the shade tree, Cleopatra started to slow down, but Cassidy spurred her on. "Sorry, girl. They won't be chasing us down today." A sob caught in her throat. "*No.*" She pulled up short. Leaning forward, she wrapped her arms around her horse's neck. "He won't do this to us again."

She felt her tears fall on Cleopatra's mane. She sat up, wiping them away. Taking a deep breath, she jumped off her horse and led the mare to the water. She stood by the bank of the stream allowing the sound of the small waterfall a few feet away to soothe the ache in her heart. She knelt and splashed water on her face. He was a memory, nothing more.

She patted Cleopatra. "We have a job to do and we aren't going to let some two-timing, double-crossing Casanova stop us."

She swung herself back into the saddle. "Let's go, girl. We have fences to check and a class to teach." Cassidy fought to get her heart under control as she rode the fence line. The smooth canter of her horse helped to calm her. At the school, she led Cleopatra to the watering trough. She rubbed her neck. "I'm not going to need you for this class. You get to relax while I teach the little ones how to rope."

"Cassidy, I'll take care of Cleo for you." She glanced up to see Pete, the foreman at the school, limp from the barn.

"Your hip hurting today?"

He patted his left hip. "Must be going to rain." He took the reins from Cassidy's hand. "You're a little early."

"Was checking fencing."

"You find more work for us to do?"

She attempted to smile. "A few boards need replacing, but not many."

"You feeling okay? You look a little pale."

"Just a headache, that's all."

"Either Carlos or I can help Alli with the class."

"Thanks, but I'm fine." She was almost to the door of the school when Pete called after her.

"Looking forward to seeing you ride the bulls this weekend."

She turned, grinning. "I'm looking forward to it, too."

Inside, she was pulling out the roping dummy when she heard the door open. Cassidy turned and saw her best friend, Allison Cartwright. Cassidy stood with her hands on her hips. "Why didn't you tell me he was coming home and..." her voice broke, "and bringing someone with him?"

"I didn't know." Allison rushed to her friend. "How did you find out?"

"I saw them." She gritted her teeth. "Driving by."

Allison hugged her friend. "Not the way we've been praying for him to come home, is it?"

Cassidy pulled away and wiped a stray tear from her cheek. "It's been five years. What did we expect?"

"If it helps, I hate her."

"That's a very strong word."

"Not strong enough." Allison grabbed one of the dummies and started pushing it to the center of the room alongside Cassidy and her roping dummy. "She didn't even say hi to my parents before she demanded to use the bathroom."

"Maybe she had to go really bad."

Allison rolled her eyes. "Doesn't excuse her being rude. When Shane told her there was one in the barn, I thought she would flip. My mother slipped her arm in hers and she pushed it away."

Cassidy gasped.

"My mother had just petted the dog and Jennifer didn't want dog hair on her."

"Oh, brother." Cassidy positioned the dummy facing Allison's. "Why would he love someone like that?"

"Love." Allison spit the word out. "He doesn't love her."

"Then why bring her home?"

"I promise you he isn't with her for love." Allison took a deep breath before whispering, "They're doing this weekend's rodeo."

"What?"

Cassidy dropped the lassos in her hands. She spun toward the office. "I have to call Mr. Scottsdale and withdraw myself."

Allison grasped Cassidy by the arm. "*No!*"

"I can't—"

"You can and you will. Stop letting him control your life." Allison picked up the ropes. "You love bull riding almost as much as you do barrel racing. It's time you stop letting him dictate how many rodeos you compete in." Allison snickered. "You need to beat him."

Cassidy closed her eyes and took a deep breath. "I can't."

"The Cassidy McDaniel I know doesn't know the meaning of the word can't." Allison hugged her friend. "You can and will do this. If not for yourself, you have to for Nancy."

Cassidy threw her hands over her face and groaned. "I hate him."

Allison grinned. "That's a strong word."

"I do, I really do."

"You trying to convince me or yourself?" Allison went back to lining up the roping dummies.

"Has your brother said anything about Divadeville?"

"Who?"

"Shane's," she made air quotes, "friend."

"No, he doesn't talk to me about Shane."

The door opened with a bang. "Hi, Miss Cassidy and Miss Allison," Timmy said as he ran into the room, followed by his mother, Janet.

"Cassidy, can I talk to you for a minute?" Janet asked.

"Sure. I wanted to talk to you too. Let's go into the office." Once the door shut behind them, Cassidy asked, "How is Tim?"

"In a lot of pain."

"I heard he's lucky to be alive."

"I married a banker, not a rodeo cowboy, like half the guys in this town." Janet twisted her hands together. "And he still almost gets killed."

Cassidy put her arms around her friend. "But he didn't."

Janet wiped the tears from her eyes. "Who would have thought a car would jump the curb and plow through the bank's window, right into Tim's desk?"

"God was watching out for him."

"I don't even want to think about what would have happened if he hadn't needed a cup of coffee."

"Praise God for coffee."

"If he had gotten that coffee a few minutes before—" Janet shivered.

Cassidy took the woman's hands in hers. "You know what-if's are the devil's way of keeping our focus off the true picture. Get them out of your mind and praise God for what did happen."

"You're so right."

"I'm praying for him to have a quick recovery."

"Thank you."

"When will he be out of the hospital?"

"Not for a while."

"If there is anything I can do to help, let me know."

"That's what I want to talk to you about. Everything will be covered by insurance, but between the car insurance and his workman's comp fighting over who pays what, it might take a few months to get settled. So, unfortunately, Timmy will not be able to continue with his classes." Janet wiped tears from her eyes. "I hate to do this, but with no money coming in, I have to cut expenses."

Cassidy touched Janet's arm. "I understand. But you don't have to stop bringing him. The school has him covered until you can afford to pay again."

"I can't ask you to do that."

"You aren't asking. It's just what the school does. Wyatt's dad got hurt pretty bad by a bull and we are doing the same for him." Cassidy reached into the front pocket of her jeans, pulled out a check, and handed it to Janet. "This is for you."

Janet looked at the thousand-dollar check and gasped. "I can't take this."

"You not only can, but you will."

"Cassidy, I can't take your money."

"It's not my money. It's from the Cowboy Fund."

"But Tim isn't a cowboy. He hates horses."

Cassidy laughed. "Never could understand how a woman who loved horses as much as you do could marry a city boy who was afraid of them."

Janet grinned. "Love is a strange thing."

"That it is."

Janet stared at the check. "What will everyone else think about this?"

"Nothing. And if they do I will just remind them how you have helped raise money for this fund since day one." Cassidy linked her arm in Janet's. "I have been thinking about changing the name from the Cowboy Fund to Neighbors in Need anyway. Last year, when Mr. Carl fell and broke his hip on the ice, we helped him and he's never been a cowboy. Or how about when we helped Belinda after she had that car accident? No one has ever complained when we help non-cowboys or girls."

Janet hugged Cassidy. "Thank you."

"If you need help with anything, you let us know. We are here."

They strolled out of the office arm in arm. Cassidy looked at Timmy twirling his rope over his head. "He might look like his dad, but definitely didn't get his father's genes."

"Thank goodness for that." Janet laughed.

Teaching a class full of five and six-year-olds to rope, kept her mind off Shane. However, the two and a half-mile ride home across the pastures after the class gave Cassidy too much time to think about Shane's homecoming. By the time she arrived, the simple act of walking Cleopatra around the paddock to cool her became a chore. Each step felt like twenty.

Cleopatra, sensing her mood, took her nose and tipped Cassidy's hat. Cassidy tried to smile. She leaned her head against the mare. "Sorry, girl. I'm not in the mood to play. But you know that, don't you?"

"Guess you heard," Hank said.

Cassidy nodded her head.

He draped his arm across her shoulders. "I tried calling, but it just kept ringing."

"You and half the town."

"That bad?"

"You have no idea. I turned my phone off."

"So, who told you? Allison?"

"I saw him driving by."

"Did he stop?"

Cassidy shook her head. "He had a wo—" her voice broke, "...a woman with him." She led Cleopatra into the barn and busied herself with unsaddling the horse.

"I heard." Her father took the saddle from her. "Maybe it's not what you think?"

Cassidy yanked the blanket off Cleopatra. "I saw her kissing him."

"While he was driving?"

Cassidy stopped mid-step. "Really, Dad."

She led her horse around to the water hose and gently hosed her down, before starting to brush her. "It's been years. What did I expect?" She knew what she expected. For five long years, she had prayed he would come home. To her. That somehow they could get past that one heart-wrenching moment. She leaned her face into Cleopatra's neck. "How could it hurt this bad?" she barely whispered. "I should be over him." She stomped her foot. "I am over him." She waved the brush in the air. "This jumble of emotions I'm feeling is just what-if's trying to worm their way into my head. It won't work. Shane Cartwright is a memory best left in the past."

"Uh huh." Hank squeezed her gently on the shoulder. "I'll finish up here. You go up to the house and talk to your mother."

"Nothing to talk about."

He took the brush from her hand. "Go."

She took the brush back. "This is what I need, to take care of my horse." She hugged Cleopatra. "Right, girl?" She ran the brush down the horse's neck. "We have been here before, haven't we? We dealt with it last time, we will this time."

"You wouldn't be so broken up about it if you had dealt with it the first time." Hank pulled her into an embrace. "One way or another, this is an answer to your prayers."

Cassidy pulled away. "How can you say that?"

"One of two things is going to happen. You get back together and all becomes right with the world, or you finally get over him. Either way, God's plan will work out."

Chapter 3

Shane shoved his pillow over his face and screamed. This trip was turning into a nightmare. In what universe had he thought it would be a good idea to bring Jennifer here? First, she hadn't been happy about the sleeping arrangements. Yes, he should have told her before they arrived, but he was a coward. Then she made a fuss about there being no alcohol in the house. For the rest of the evening, she had been sulking. Worse yet, his parents had kept looking at him with disappointment.

He took a deep breath before punching the pillow and putting it behind his head. Laying back, he couldn't help but glance at the rodeo poster of a seventeen-year-old Cassidy hanging on his wall. Sapphire eyes looked accusingly at him. *"You brought a woman home,"* they seemed to scream at him. He groaned and rolled over. He never should have come.

He had barely closed his eyes when he heard the door creak open. The light from the hall illuminated Jennifer in a sheer nightgown. "You can't be in here," he said.

She tiptoed to the bed. "Shh, scoot over."

Shane jumped up, grabbed her by the arm, and pulled her toward the door. "You can't be in here."

Jennifer laughed. "Stop being such a boy scout." She pulled her arm free and hurried to the bed. "I'll be gone before anyone wakes up."

"No." He started to open the door.

Jennifer crawled under the covers. "Come on, baby." She patted the bed.

"Jennifer, you can't be in here."

"Why not?"

"I will not disrespect my parents' house."

"You don't mind disrespecting my parents."

"Your parents don't think it's a sin."

Jennifer laughed. "And neither do you." Jennifer flipped the covers off. "Oh, I get it. 'God' only sees things at your parents' house." She flipped her long blonde hair over her shoulder. As she stood, her hand brushed the light and it turned on. She started to run her hand down the front of her sheer negligée. "Tell me you don't—What—" She dashed across the room and waved her arms wildly. "What is this doing here?"

"It's a poster."

"I see that, you idiot." Jennifer spun on him. "I want to know why it's here."

"Jennifer, calm down."

"Calm down! You have your ex plastered on your walls and you want me to calm down?"

"I haven't been home in five years. I never got around to taking it down."

Jennifer reached up and snatched it off the wall. Shane watched in horror as Cassidy's face ripped in two.

He grabbed Jennifer's hands. "Stop it."

"What is going on here?" His mother's voice froze him in place. "Why is she in your room?"

"It's not what it looks like."

"Really, you in your underwear, her barely dressed." Ann took her bathrobe off and tossed it to Jennifer. "Put that on before someone else sees everything the good Lord gave you."

Jennifer held the fuzzy bathrobe at arm's length. "I'm..."

"Now!"

Jennifer quickly obeyed.

"Young lady, there are rules in this house. Rules you were informed of before you came prancing in here." Ann pointed to the door. "You are to return to your room and unless it's to use the bathroom, you will not leave it until morning. Do not let me see you parading my halls dressed in nothing again. Is that understood?"

Jennifer nodded as she inched her way out the door. She glared at Shane. "This is not over." She stormed down the hall, slamming her door behind her.

"Well, if everyone wasn't awake, they are now." Shane attempted to smile.

"Put on some jeans and meet me in the kitchen."

Shane nodded as his mother left the room. He stared at the tattered face of Cassidy laying at his feet. A lump swelled in his throat as he picked up the pieces and hugged them to his chest. This was what he had done to them, shredded their love until there was nothing left but a memory. His heart clenched, taking his breath away. He fell to his knees. This wasn't the way it was supposed to be. One stupid mistake had led him to this.

He picked himself up, gently laying the torn pieces of the poster on his bed. His fingers brushed across them. "I'm sorry." He wiped a tear from his eye, pulled on his jeans, and grabbed a shirt. Time to face the music.

Jennifer slammed the door, not caring who she woke up. Served this stupid house and the backward people in it right. Did they really believe in a book that was thousands of years old? She paced the floor. What were they supposed to do here at night anyway? It was barely after nine and everyone was in bed. She kicked his mother's robe across the room. Bet they were having sex. She threw a shoe at the door. Not likely—under that awful robe was an even uglier flannel nightgown. Flannel in the spring. Was she crazy?

Jennifer picked up the purple, fuzzy robe off the floor with two fingers, barely touching the corner. She cautiously opened the door and peeked out before hanging the robe on the outside knob. She didn't want that thing in her room giving her bad vibes all night.

She flopped down on the bed, covered her face in the pillow, and screamed. She needed a drink. She needed sex. What she didn't need was this archaic family. She peeked out from the pillow. On the nightstand sat a Bible. She screamed again at the sight of it.

Had she picked the wrong one? Was it a mistake coming here? No, no matter who she had picked, she had to come to the town-that-time-forgot with its obsolete way of thinking. It was the only way she was going to see what would soon be hers. She snickered. Well, not totally... he did have siblings. She got up and went to the window peering out into the night. The moon hadn't risen enough to illuminate much, but she knew that way into the darkness the Cartwright lands went on and on.

She had thought her father had land, but his four hundred acres were nothing compared to the Cartwrights' thousand, and that was just their land. It didn't include the thousand-plus acres they shared with the McDaniels up in the mountains. The minute she had heard her father talking about the Cartwrights and the McDaniels, she knew she had to marry one of their sons. The only question was whether she wanted the horseman or the cattle rancher. Not that it mattered. Once the I Dos were said, she would never live on another filthy, stinky ranch again.

It would not be easy, but the riches, in the end, would be worth the troubles. So she had dusted off her boots and gone with her father to the rodeo in Boulder, where he had introduced her to both Shane Cartwright and Jake McDaniel. She smiled to herself. The fact that they were both handsome had been a pleasant surprise. Little did her father know, he had become a pawn in her plan. After pretending to be enthralled by the barrel racers, she had talked her father into hiring one of them to teach her. She hadn't cared which man she married.

They were both handsome and rich. Shane stepped into her trap.

It wasn't that hard to pretend to love him. After all, he had the charm women longed for. And his smile, when he chose to flash it, could melt any woman's heart with his big dimples and brown eyes that sparkled like hidden gems. Let's not forget the first time he had taken his shirt off she almost swooned—his six-pack abs, graced with perfectly placed dark hair all over his chest. His looks, his body, all of that was just a bonus that would earn her the envy of all her friends. What they wouldn't know was the real treasure was this ranch and the money it brought in. She pressed her face to the window, straining to see beyond the dark. Tomorrow she would see just what the Cartwrights owned. And if this didn't work out, there was always Jake McDaniel right next door.

She flopped down on the bed and pulled the covers over her shoulders. She hit her pillow. It had better be worth all this trouble. Until she talked him into marrying her, she was stuck pretending to care about horses, barrel racing, and good old country air. She groaned. She hated the foul-smelling country; she wanted to move to the city and never again have to smell horse or cow crap.

Getting him to fall for her had been easy. The hard part would be to get him to take his share and move to Denver, or maybe New York. Leaving this place wouldn't be the problem. He didn't even like it here. Otherwise, he wouldn't have been away so long. The problem would be pulling him from the rodeo and his stinking horse. She hit the pillow again. She hated that horse.

Chapter 4

"Well son, you weren't the only one that had a visitor last night." Jason squeezed Shane's shoulder.

He scowled at Jennifer. "Who else?"

Jason took his seat at the head of the table. "Just got off the phone with Hank. Seems Antony took a midnight stroll to see his lady."

Shane pushed his chair back so fast it almost fell over.

"Sit back down. He's okay. Someone will bring him home after breakfast."

"Shane," Jennifer grabbed his arm, "you have to go get him."

Jason reached for the plate of French toast. "Not necessary." He placed a couple of pieces on his plate before passing it around the table.

"But Shane's the only one that can handle that horse."

"He's not the only one," Shane's brother Luke said, passing the plate to Jennifer.

"Who else can?" Jennifer asked

"Cassidy," Allison said with a grin.

"The ex-girlfriend?"

Someone said, "Yup." With a little too much pleasure.

Jennifer dropped her fork. "She can't!" She started to rise. "We need to go get him."

"We?"

"That woman is not coming here," she shrieked.

"Of course she is, she comes here all the time," Ann said.

"I won't allow it."

"Young lady, you might be a guest in this house, but that does not give you the right to say who or what is allowed here," Jason said with a smile, but his eyes told a different story.

"Don't worry, I'll ride out to meet her." Shane started to rise.

"I'm going with you."

"That isn't necessary."

"You are not going to be alone with that woman." She stared at him. "I will not allow it."

"Not allow it!" Allison glared at Jennifer before looking across at her brother. "Really?"

"Everyone calm down," Ann said.

"Can we please say grace before the food gets cold?" Jason bowed his head. "Good morning, Father. We thank You for this wonderful day and the food we are about to eat. Let this day bring nothing we can't handle in a Godly manner, and if it does, please give us the strength to deal with it. Amen." He jabbed his fork into his French toast and took a big bite. "Mighty tasty as always." He winked at his wife. "God sure did bless me when he brought you into my life."

Ann grinned. "He sure did." Laughter filled the room.

Allison's phone dinged. She pulled it from her back pocket.

"You know the rules," her father said. "No phones at the table."

Allison pushed her chair back. "Be right back. This is important."

"Antony, you naughty boy," Cassidy said kissing his nose. "It's so good to see you." He nuzzled her arm, trying to reach into her pocket. "Aww, you remember where I keep the treats." She reached in and pulled out two apples. She held out her hands and let Antony and Cleopatra gobble them up.

When they were finished, she turned from the horses, pulled out her phone, and texted Allison.

Hey, I'm bringing Antony home in a few minutes. Don't let Shane come.

The reply came quickly.

How do you think I can stop him?

She sent a frown emoji.

Then come with him. Pleeeeease.

Allison replied with a thumbs up.

Returning to the horses, Cassidy said, "Sorry, you two love birds, but I need to break this up." She rubbed both horses' necks. "I know it's hard, but you will see each other soon. I promise." She led Cleopatra into the barn and saddled her before putting a lead rope on Antony. "Time to get this over with."

Her father held the gate open. He ran his hand down the silver horse's back. Antony side-stepped and curled his lips at him. Hank pulled his hand away quickly. "Yeah, I know. Only two people can touch you and I'm not one of them."

Cassidy was almost to the stream when her stomach filled with butterflies. Her eyes drifted toward their tree. A few seconds later she saw the crown of his white Stetson top the hill, followed by the rest of him. Her heart felt as if it was going to jump from her chest. She put her hand over her heart. She waited for Allison to follow behind him, but she didn't see her. This wasn't happening. Cassidy couldn't be alone with him. She reined her horse to a stop and pulled out her phone.

Where are you?

Allison quickly responded.

A few minutes behind.

Cassidy stayed where she was, searching the horizon for her friend.

Hurry up. I can't be alone with him.

As fast as Shane was moving, it wouldn't take him long to reach them. She placed the lead rope across Antony's shoulders and gave him a little push. "Go." Antony refused to move. "Go." She nudged him with her foot. He swung his head around and snorted at her. "Come on. You know that didn't hurt." She pointed at Shane. "Look. There's Shane and he's riding your son, Caesar. Go get him." Antony looked at her. "Please go." He neighed and shook his head. "Antony, you know what he did to me." A sob caught in her throat. "I can't do this. Please go."

The horse slightly nodded and took a step forward before turning to look at her. Cassidy leaned over and kissed the top of his head. "Go." Antony took off toward Shane. Cassidy tried to turn Cleopatra back home, but she refused to budge.

"Come on. We have to go."

Cleopatra shook her head. It took all of Cassidy's strength to force the horse toward home. Cassidy spurred Cleopatra on.

"Cassidy, wait." The rich baritone of his voice filled her with a longing she thought she had forgotten. She urged her mare faster.

Too late, Shane's hand grabbed hold of Cleopatra's reins and she was once again gazing into the face she was only allowed to see in her dreams. The strong jawline with his morning stubble, those rich brown eyes with flecks of gold, the dimples she knew were there but hidden at the moment, all caused an orchestra of butterflies to flutter through her. Seeing him was like a warm summer rain after a long drought to her soul. It was all she could do to stay in the saddle and not throw herself into his arms. Like a rattlesnake, her brain slithered around her heart shouting, *"Run. He's a traitor. He can't be trusted. Run."*

It took every ounce of breath to say, "Let go of her."

"Cassidy, we need to talk."

"No. We don't."

"Please."

"Let go of my horse." Cassidy looked over her shoulder. Relief flooded her at the sight of Allison and Shane's new woman. "Looks like your girlfriend is here. Now let go."

"Cassidy, it's been five years. Why won't you talk to me?"

"Five years or a thousand, doesn't matter." She pointed to the woman beside Allison. "She proves you have nothing to say that I want to hear." Cassidy jabbed her heels into Cleopatra's side and took off at a run. It wasn't until she rode over the hill and was out of sight of the others that she slowed down. The sound of horse's hooves pounding the ground behind her sent a sliver of dread through her. She turned in the saddle. Relief flooded her at the sight of her friend.

"Didn't you hear me calling you?" Allison said riding up beside her. "The way you were riding, I thought the devil was after you."

"Close."

Allison put her hands on her waist. "My brother is not close to the devil. Now his girlfriend, that's another story."

"She can't be that bad?"

Allison huffed. "You have no idea."

"Shane loves," Cassidy stumbled over the word, "her..."

"Whoa, he doesn't love her."

"Then why bring her home?"

Allison rolled her eyes. "Jennifer is hoping to get enough barrel racing points to qualify for the WPRA Finals."

"What?" Cassidy groaned. "She's competing this weekend?"

"Yup."

"Can this weekend get any worse?"

Allison giggled and gently punched Cassidy's arm. "It'll be great once we beat her."

"Maybe she's good."

"Huh. The prima donna can't even saddle her own horse." Allison fanned her hand. "She might break a nail."

"What?"

"That's what took so long. Miss Divadeville refused to saddle the horse. Luckily, Luke came in and did it. Otherwise, we would never have made it."

"How is that possible?"

"She said a stable hand or Shane always does it."

"What about at the rodeo?"

"Her father sends a stable hand with her."

"Why would Shane want to be with someone like that?"

"I have no idea." Allison grabbed Cassidy's arm. "You have to save him."

"Are you crazy?"

"He isn't happy."

"That has nothing to do with me."

"It has everything to do with you. Ever since the two of you broke up, neither of you have been happy. You need to get back together."

"Allison, we've had this conversation too many times to be having it again."

"But—"

"I will say this one more time. He can't be trusted. Without trust, there is nothing. End of story."

Chapter 5

Shane stood at the bar waiting for his pitcher of beer and Jennifer's wine.

"So the prodigal idiot has returned."

He braced for the slap on the back he knew was coming from his best friend, Jake McDaniel.

"Who are you calling an idiot?"

"You."

"Why? What did I do?"

Jake glanced across the room to the long table where their friends were starting to gather. He nodded toward Jennifer. "For starters, bringing her here."

"What was I supposed to do, leave her at my parents' house?"

Jake closed his eyes and shook his head. "You are a simpleton, aren't you? I'm talking about you haven't been home in five years and when you finally return you bring her." Jake glanced out of the corner of his eye toward Jennifer.

"We've been dating for almost a year. Why wouldn't I bring her?"

Jake rubbed the back of his neck. "You are clueless, aren't you?" He punched Shane in the arm. "You bring a woman home to meet Momma and she and everyone else expects to see a ring."

"Are you crazy?"

Jake threw his hands up. "Not me. I know the deal. But the rumor is going around that you're about to pop the question." Jake grinned and leaned back on his heels. "Maybe now Cassidy will give one of these lonely cowboys a chance."

"They better stay away from her."

Jake punched Shane in the arm. "You, my friend, gave up the right to say that a long time ago." He glanced around the room. "How did it go this morning?"

"She refused to talk to me."

"Can't say I blame her this time. You did bring a woman home to meet your mother."

"I didn't bring her home to meet my mother. I brought her here to compete in the rodeo this weekend."

Jake laughed. "You mean to get beat?"

Shane grinned. "Yeah."

"You know for the life of me, I can't figure it out."

"What?"

"You and my sister were the perfect couple. And not only did you blow it, you never fought to get her back."

"Obviously we weren't meant to be together."

Jake stared at his friend dumbfounded. "Did a bull kick you in the head or something?"

"No."

"Then you're a moron."

"What is it with you?"

Jake grabbed his beer and took a big swig. "It's been one thing to watch you jump from woman to woman trying to pretend you're over Cassidy. When you and I know you aren't."

"I..."

Jake held up his hand. "Don't add lying to your list of sins. What you two had, most people only dream about. But the connection you two have, now that is beyond this world."

"We didn't have a connection."

"Oh really? What about that time when in the middle of English class, you jumped up and ran out. When Mrs. Cole told you to sit back down, you said Cassidy was in trouble. And if you hadn't jumped in your car and sped off to town, Cassidy and my mother would have drowned when their car was swept off the bridge into the river."

Shane shivered. "Just luck."

"You know better. What about that time we were out riding and that snow squall came out of nowhere? Somehow Cassidy led my father right to us. Otherwise, we would have frozen to death."

"Whatever that connection was, it's gone now."

"Oh really? Remember when you broke your collarbone when you were tossed from a bull a few years ago?"

Shane rubbed his shoulder. "How could I forget?"

"Explain how Cassidy was rounding the third barrel two states over and she knocked it over."

"She knocked over a barrel?"

Jake nodded.

"She wasn't riding Cleopatra—"

"She was."

"Impossible."

"She lost focus because somehow she knew you were hurt. She rushed over to Allison and made her call your mother to find out."

"I didn't know that." Shane's heart skipped a beat. He could feel every inch of his body stilling. Without turning, he knew she had just walked in.

"Huh. Don't tell me you still don't feel that connection. I can see it on your face. You know Cassidy is here." Jake laid his hand on his friend's arm. "And she feels it too. She knew exactly where you were the second she opened the door. So, my friend, what are you going to do about it?"

"It has nothing to do with a connection. More like the sudden quiet in the place."

"Everyone knows it's the first time in five years you two have been in the same room together. And we're all wondering what's going to happen."

Shane rubbed his forehead. "Nothing is going to happen. She won't talk to me." Shane looked in the mirror at the face he had tried to forget, the face of an angel. His heart pounded, drowning out the noise around him.

She was more beautiful than he remembered. If that was possible. Her white dress had tiny pink dots all over it, hugged her tiny waist, then flared out to just below her knees. She wore simple jewelry, a necklace, and earrings. Her black hair flowed loose around her shoulders. Even from this distance, the blue of her eyes was like a siren of the sea inviting him to come to her. For a moment, he did just that, a warm glow spreading through him. Then, like a steel trap, the warmth of her eyes slammed shut and was replaced with cold steel. He felt a shiver go through him. Seconds before, he felt a cold wet kiss on his neck.

"What is taking so long?"

"My fault," Jake said. "I was talking to him."

Jennifer took a long sip of wine. "I needed that," she said to Jake. "Can you believe his parents don't allow alcohol of any kind in their house?"

"Yup."

"How about your parents? Alcohol allowed there?"

"Occasionally."

"It's a wonder they allow their children to come to a bar."

"My parents do not control what we do or where we go."

Jake mumbled under his breath. "That's obvious."

Jennifer rolled her eyes. She linked her arm with Shane's and nodded toward the table. "Come on, I want to meet your friends."

Jake laughed. "I'm the only one that matters."

Shane punched his arm. "You keep believing that." Together, the three of them went back to the table. Shane looked around. So far, Cassidy had yet to join the group. His heart dropped. She was dancing with Luke. He watched as she leaned against the other man's chest. He pushed the slow burn of betrayal down and flopped in his seat. Was she dating his brother? How could she?

The second the door opened her eyes drifted right to him. For a minute, his gaze locked with hers and all seemed right with the world. Then the blonde seductress sizzled up to mark her territory. Like a harpoon to the heart, the pain of rejection swept through her. Cassidy spun to leave.

A firm hand grabbed her by the arm. "Oh no, you don't." She glanced over her shoulder at a younger version of Shane, his brother Luke. "I'm going to ask you what you asked me a few months ago when Mandy came waltzing in with her new boyfriend. Are you a cowboy or a buttercup?"

"I'm not a cowboy."

"No, you aren't." Luke grinned. "Let me rephrase that. Are you a cowgirl or a buttercup?"

Softly she said, "A buttercup."

Luke led her to the dance floor. "Well, buck up, buttercup."

Cassidy couldn't stop the giggle that snuck out.

"This isn't going to be an easy ride."

"I shouldn't have come."

"And yet, you did."

She leaned her forehead against his chest. "What was I thinking?"

"Listen, I know this hurts. The first time seeing them together is always the hardest. But I have seen you handle tougher things than this."

"I don't think so."

He squeezed her softly. "I think you're right. But you got this." The music stopped and they headed off the dance floor. Luke took her hand in his. "You ready to face the real music?"

"Not really." She took a deep breath. "Could you pull the dagger out of my heart first?"

He shook his head. "Only two people on this earth can do that for you and I'm not one of them."

"I wish I knew how."

"By forgiving him?"

Cassidy stopped mid-step. "Forgiving him is the easy part. It's the trusting I can't do."

"I've been saying this for years and I'm going to say it again. What he did was wrong, but was it really worth five years of misery?" Luke spun her around. "There are dozens of cowboys just waiting for the green light with you. Either figure a way to forgive him or move on." Luke kissed her on the cheek. "You know I love you like a sister, and he is my brother, which means seeing the two of you like this hurts me almost as much as it does the two of you."

"The two of us?" Cassidy nodded toward them. Jennifer's blonde head was on Shane's shoulder. She was snuggled so close to him she might as well have been in his lap. "Looks to me like one of us is doing just fine."

"Don't let looks deceive you."

At the table, the only chair left was across from Shane and Jennifer. No way was she sitting there. Going to the far end of the table, Cassidy grabbed a chair from behind her and pushed her brother, Ben, down a little. "Hey, there's an empty—" He nodded down at the end of the table before realizing who was there. "Never mind." He squeezed her leg. "Going to be a wild night."

"You think?"

Ben whispered in her ear, "Have you met her?"

Cassidy lowered her head. "Do I have to?"

Ben bumped his shoulder against hers. "She has nothing on you."

"Good for her. Because what I had was never good enough."

"He was a fool. You are more than good enough."

Allison left her seat across from her brother and went to the end of the table with Cassidy. "Hey, you all, move down one." Without hesitation, the four on their side did.

"Thank you," Cassidy said.

Allison leaned over and whispered, "No way was I going to sit across from Divadeville all night."

The owner of the diner came up behind Cassidy and placed water filled with fruit in front of her. She winked. "I figured you needed something more than a twist of lemon."

Cassidy grinned. "Thanks."

Rita's knees cracked as she knelt beside Cassidy and whispered, "You want me to take him out behind the woodshed?"

Cassidy giggled. "Tempting, but no. It's been five years. Everything is okay."

"Poosh," Rita said. "I saw the look on your face and his when you walked in. You can't fool me." Standing, Rita said to the others, "Your usual?" Everyone said, "Yes." She moved down to the end of the table. "About time you got the courage to drag your sorry tail home."

Shane went around to the other side of the table and threw his arms around the elderly woman, lifting her off the ground in a big bear hug. "Nice to see you, too."

"Put me down. Your Don Juan ways don't work on me," she said with a grin.

Shane kissed her on the cheek. "Sure they do."

She tried not to laugh. Instead, she swatted him on the arm. "Get back around there before I have to call the bouncer on you." Rita nodded at the drinks in front of them. "You two okay?"

Shane nodded. "For now."

"Speak for yourself. I would like another glass of wine." When Rita left their table, Jennifer said, "What were you thinking, flirting with that rude woman?"

"She wasn't rude."

"Did you hear what she said to you?"

"That was just her way of saying welcome home."

"Humph. I have half a mind to report her to the manager."

"Might be hard to do, since she and her husband own the place."

"How do they keep customers with her being so ill-mannered?"

"She's harmless." Shane took a big swig of beer before making the introduction around the table. "You know Jake, Tanner, and Rosemary from the rodeos, and of course Luke and Allison. Those you don't know are Joelle, Ben McDaniel, and—"

Jennifer smiled sweetly at Ben. "Oh, I didn't know there was another handsome McDaniel brother."

Shane started to introduce Cassidy. Jennifer quickly turned her head and leaned in, kissing Shane before he could say her name.

Cassidy wanted to puke. She took a deep breath, stilling the turmoil inside her. Ben squeezed her hand. She gave her brother a weak smile. She reached in her purse and pulled out a small leather pouch.

Allison leaned toward her. "Are you going to get Shane's keys?"

Cassidy grumbled. "I have to. He's drinking."

Allison grinned. "So you'll have to talk to him."

"Unfortunately." Cassidy stood up. "Okay, you guys know the drill. Give me your keys." She walked behind the chairs. Everyone willingly dropped their keys into her pouch. When she got to the end of the table, she held the pouch out to Shane.

"You still doing this?"

"Obviously."

When he pulled the keys from his pocket, Jennifer nearly choked on her wine. "Why are you giving her the keys to your truck? You won't even let me touch it."

Jake laughed. "It's your boyfriend's fault she takes our keys."

Jennifer looked at Shane.

Jake continued. "On Shane's twenty-first birthday he got a little out of hand. When Cassidy tried to get the keys from him, he refused to give them to her. He picked her up, put her in the front seat, jumped in beside her, and took off, driving a hundred miles an hour. Cassidy was screaming for him to stop. Of course, being the idiot he was, he didn't. Until he happened to glance over and see the fear on her face. I know this is true because I was in the back seat, holding on for dear life. When he finally pulled over, Cassidy jumped out of the truck and took off running. We searched for her, but couldn't find her. After twenty minutes, his father and brother showed up and drove us home. That was the longest Cassidy ever went without talking to him."

"Not the longest," Shane whispered, looking straight at Cassidy.

"After that, she started collecting our keys when we got here. And we only get them back if she thinks we're okay to drive. If not, she drives us home."

"Stop." Jennifer pulled Shane's hand back from the bag. "I can't believe you allow her to treat you like children."

"Everyone at this table knows she's doing it because she cares," Allison said coming up beside Cassidy.

"Well, I'm glad I have the man and not the foolish boy." Jennifer leaned her head on Shane's shoulder. "A man that doesn't need some girl telling him what he can and cannot do."

"Fool is an understatement," Jake said. Shane glared at him.

Cassidy dangled her bag in front of Jake. "If you are finished with telling stories, I'll take your keys." Jake dropped his keys into the bag. She held it out to Shane.

When he dropped his keys in, Jennifer huffed. "Really?"

"Yes. Really." Shane stood up. "I need some fresh air."

Cassidy resisted the urge to follow. But five minutes later she was ready to run out the door. That was all it took to see a paper doll had more substance than Jennifer. What did he see in that woman? There was no way this temptress was in love with Shane. From the moment the door had shut behind him, she had done nothing but flirt with the other men at the table, mainly Jake and Ben.

Ben grabbed Joelle's hand. "Let's dance."

Jake tried to ignore her, but Jennifer was not going to be snubbed. She went to the other side of the table and sat right down on his lap. He jumped up so fast, he nearly knocked the whole table over. Everyone grabbed their drinks before they were wearing them. "Are you crazy?" Jake darted around Jennifer and went out the back door. A few minutes later, he and Shane returned.

The evening dragged on. If not for her friends keeping her dancing and laughing, Cassidy would have never made it through the night. She was glad she didn't have to drive anyone home. She was emotionally wiped out. As she pulled around the driveway, her headlights caught a streak of silver. She couldn't help but smile as she watched Antony jump the fence. She picked up her phone and dialed Allison. "Hey, I have a midnight visitor."

"Again?"

"Tell Shane not to bother coming to get him in the morning. I'll bring him to the rodeo with Cleopatra." She hung up and opened the half gate into the paddock. Antony turned his head and looked at her. "What am I going to do with you?" She ran her hand along his body as he turned toward the barn. It came away wet. "I know you miss her. But this isn't your home."

He nuzzled her neck. "I know we promised you two would be together." She sighed. "But things don't always work out the way we plan." She grabbed him by the halter. "Going to have to cool you down before you get to see your lady." She talked while she led him. "You know it's five miles across the fields. That is a long way for you to be running in the middle of the night." She leaned her head against his. "It's not safe. There are wolves, coyotes, bears, and who knows what else lurking out there in the dark. You need to stop doing this." She sighed. "Guess we don't have to worry about that anymore after tonight. The rodeo starts tomorrow and you and Cleopatra will be together all weekend. Then you go back home." Her heart clenched. She wasn't sure if it was the thought of seeing Shane and Jennifer all weekend or the thought of watching him drive away once again.

She led the stallion to the stall beside Cleopatra. He whinnied and poked his head over the divider. Cleopatra whinnied back. "We have a busy weekend ahead, so you two get some rest." She closed the barn door and went into the house. She was surprised her mother, Rachel, was still up.

"Heard you pull in. What took you so long?"

"Antony is back."

Rachel shook her head. "That stallion knows what he wants. Doesn't he?"

"They've been apart for too long."

"That they have." Rachel handed her a piece of cake. "Thought you might need some chocolate."

Cassidy grinned. "You know me so well."

"How was it?"

"Uneventful. Unless you want to count all twenty times Jennifer kissed Shane." Cassidy took a big bite of cake. "Not that I counted."

"Twenty times?"

"Yup. She was all over him. Kissing him when they were dancing, kissing him every time he got up to leave the table, kissing him when he came back."

Her mother raised an eyebrow. "And it matters to you, why?"

"It doesn't."

"Humph." She looked Cassidy straight in the eyes. "Love is a terrible thing to waste."

"Love died a long time ago."

Chapter 6

"Why am I in the slack, while they..." Jennifer pointed at Cassidy's and Allison's names on the program, "...get a free pass to ride tonight?"

"Be in the top ten today and you'll ride tonight, too."

"Why don't they have to qualify?"

"They were last year's winner and runner up, so they get a free pass from the slack this year."

"I never heard of such a thing."

"That's just the way it's done here in Berksville. Win this year and you automatically get a free pass out of the slack rounds."

Jennifer folded her arms across her chest and stomped her foot. "Well, I don't like it."

"Too bad." He started to walk away, then stopped. He waved his arm in the direction of the other barrel racers. "Do you see anyone else having a hissy fit over being in the slack? No! Because that's the way it is. I'm in the slack for team roping, bull riding, and calf roping. Do you see me complaining? No. And for that matter, Jake has to be in there with me, even though he and Ben won team roping last year. But I wasn't here, so he has to be in the slack with me. Is he complaining?"

"How would I know? I haven't talked to him."

"Well, I promise you he isn't. So get over yourself."
He stormed off.

At the pens, he watched Cassidy working hard alongside her father and brothers herding the broncos from the trailer into the pens. Something you wouldn't catch Jennifer doing for a million bucks. He internally groaned. The only thing similar about the two of them was that they were both raised on a ranch, and barrel raced. And of course, they were both beautiful. Who was he kidding? Jennifer's fake beauty was nothing compared to the natural beauty of Cassidy. Cassidy's true beauty shone from the inside out, while Jennifer's was only skin-deep.

What did he ever see in Jennifer? His brain smacked himself. He knew why. Being with someone opposite of Cassidy kept her memory buried deep. Only it didn't work. A memory like her always found a way back into his dreams.

"Hey," Luke said, slapping Shane on the back. "You going to stare at her all day or you going to come help us with the bulls?"

Just as he was about to turn, Cassidy glanced his way. She quickly looked away. His heart sank. Would there ever come a day when she didn't look at him with eyes full of agony?

"I understand we are in for a treat," the announcer said. "This might be her rookie season, but she has been raking in the points. Jennifer Martin, you're up."

Cassidy and Allison stood along the fence line watching. "You think she's any good?"

"I trained her, didn't I?" Shane said, slipping up behind them. He leaned on the fence beside Cassidy, smiling. Without hesitation, she moved to the other side.

"Don't you think you should have told her not to wear boots with heels on them?" Allison asked.

"I tried."

Jennifer entered the ring. Within seconds she was flying around the barrels. The second barrel teetered but didn't fall. The crowd went wild when her time flashed on the board—15.39 seconds. The announcer said, "We have a new leader."

Jennifer rode over to where they were standing. Cassidy started to say, "Great—"

"Beat that," Jennifer interrupted, flipping her long blonde hair over her shoulder then rode off.

Cassidy turned to leave. "I have work to do."

Shane started to follow her. Allison grabbed him by the arm. "No."

He jerked his arm away and started walking. Allison grabbed him again. "I said, 'no'. For five years, I have tried to get you to come home and straighten things out with her, but no. You couldn't do that. And when you finally do come home, you come dragging Divadeville with you. And if that isn't bad enough, you are chasing after Cassidy like a dog in heat."

"I just want to talk to her."

"Stop chasing her."

"I need—"

"You need your head examined."

Shane grinned. "You're right. I do." He tipped his hat back a little on his head. "How do I fix things with Cassidy if she won't even talk to me?"

"It's never going to happen as long as you're with Divadeville. You just keep proving to Cassidy that you haven't changed at all. You are still the man that thinks kissing another woman is no big deal."

"It wasn't even a real kiss."

"See? You still don't get it." She poked him in the chest. "Listen to your heart instead of whatever it is you're listening to." She watched as Jennifer came storming toward them. "She doesn't look happy."

Shane groaned. "No, she doesn't."

"I should have known you'd be here. Where is she?"

"Who?"

"Oh, don't play stupid with me. I know you were with her instead of being with me for my interview."

"What interview?"

"Exactly. You don't know because you were too busy with your ex."

"For your information, he's been talking to me." Allison crossed her arms in front of her chest. "Do you have a problem with him talking to his sister?"

Jennifer ignored her. She leaned into Shane, toying with the pearl buttons of his flannel shirt. "I was disappointed you weren't with me for my interview."

He took her hands off him. "Jennifer, where is Lightning?"

"I tied him to the back of the trailer."

"What?" Horrified, Shane took off running. "You know better." When he rounded the corner to the corral, he saw Cassidy walking Jennifer's horse. Jennifer was a few steps behind him.

"What are you doing with my horse?" Jennifer yelled.

"What you should have been doing." Cassidy glared at Shane. "Would have thought you taught her about taking care of her horse."

Jennifer yanked the reins from Cassidy. "You can't just walk someone else's horse."

"You can if you see the horse hurting." Cassidy rubbed Lightning's neck. "He just ran his heart out for you and this is how you repay him?"

Jennifer moved Lightning away from Cassidy. "In the future, stay away from my horse."

"In the future, take care of him and I won't have to."

Jennifer smiled. "Oh, cut the act. We all know you're just trying to impress Shane."

Cassidy gave a halting laugh. "I didn't do it for you or him." She almost spit the words out. "I did it for your horse." Cassidy patted Lightning's neck. "You did good, boy. You don't deserve to be treated like this." She started to walk away, then turned and looked at Shane. Without saying a word, she shook her head and left. The disappointment in her eyes were words enough.

"The nerve of some people." Jennifer flipped her hair and handed Lightning's reins to Shane. "I'm going over to the hotel. It's too hot here."

"You'll be wasting your time. The Grand will be all booked up."

"I already booked our room."

"When did you do that?"

"The same time I booked Billy's room."

"Billy is coming?"

Jennifer stared at him for a minute. "Of course he's coming. And if I had known I was riding this morning and not tonight, he would have flown in last night."

"I don't understand why you booked a room. That's what the trailer is for."

Jennifer gave a short laugh. "If you think for one minute I would be sleeping with horses, you are sadly mistaken."

"I figured you would go back to the ranch with my mother."

"Why would I want to do that? She hates me."

"She doesn't hate you."

Jennifer ran her hand down the front of Shane's shirt. "Why don't you come with me? I've been lonely without you these past two nights."

Shane moved Jennifer's hands from him. "Can't. I have a lot to do helping my father."

"You don't work for him." She stomped her foot. "You work for *my* father." She nuzzled in close. "A little afternoon delight will put the smile back on your face and get you out of the grumpy mood you've been in ever since we got to this..." She waved her hand around. "...this nowhere town."

"Jennifer, I have things to do." Shane stepped back from her. "You know I agreed to help my family with the stock."

"Who else are you helping?"

"What is that supposed to mean?"

"It means I know why you're really hanging around."

"You know nothing."

"You and everyone think she's so great." Jennifer poked her finger in his chest. "You just wait and see who the better woman is." Jennifer spun around and stormed off.

"We don't have to see," he mumbled under his breath.

Allison came up behind him and slipped her arm in his. "Well, now you'll be able to enjoy the day."

Shane grinned. It was only a few minutes before Jennifer was back.

"You have to drive me to the hotel."

"It's across the street. You can walk."

Jennifer glanced at the long gravel driveway. "It's not just across the street. And what about my suitcase? I can't carry it that far. You have to drive me."

"You expect me to drive my truck pulling the horse trailer from here to there?" He pointed at the hotel. "You know the temporary corral is hooked to the trailer, don't you? So while I drive you across the street all our horses get out."

Jennifer looked at Allison. "Do you have a car?"

"No. I drove one of the trailers."

Jennifer pulled out her phone. "They do have Uber in this one-horse town, don't they?"

Shane stared at her speechless. "You can't be serious?"

"I'm not walking."

"You can see it from here."

Jennifer stomped her foot. "I am not walking."

Shane shook his head and stormed off. Allison couldn't hold in the snicker. Shane glared at her. "Don't say a word."

Chapter 7

The opening ceremonies had ended and the breakaway roping event was about to start. Shane sneaked away from Jennifer so he could watch Cassidy compete. He found a quiet spot by the sheep pen. It wasn't the best spot in the world, but it was one where he could enjoy watching without having to listen to any snippy commentary. He just wanted to be alone.

He never realized until this moment how much he missed watching her. Who was he kidding? He hadn't been able to watch any of the women's events for the last five years, not even Jennifer's, because he couldn't stop wishing it was Cassidy out there.

The gate opened, releasing the calf from the chute. Cassidy and Cleopatra left the box a few seconds later. Cassidy swirled the rope over her head twice before lassoing the calf. Cleopatra came to a dead stop and the string holding the rope to the horn of the saddle broke. Shane held his breath, waiting for her time. His heart swelled with pride when 2.5 seconds flashed on the scoreboard. She was at the top of her game. No wonder she was the all-around Women's Professional Champion.

Cassidy glanced his way. His heart skipped a beat. No way she could see him here in this dark corner. Just in case, he tipped his hat to her. He stood there watching her ride out of the ring.

He turned at the sound of voices. He watched as a group of six boys ducked into the walkway. Five of them had circled a smaller boy. This wasn't going to be good. He heard one of them say, "You're just a scaredy-cat. Bet you still wear diapers." Then that person pushed a younger boy, about five, to the ground. The group around them laughed.

"Hey." Shane reached down and helped the young boy up. "What's going on here?"

"The baby is afraid to ride the sheep."

"And that gives you the right to push him?" Shane kneeled beside the boy. "What's your name, cowboy?"

"He ain't no cowboy," the bully said shoving his hands in his pockets. "He's a little baby. Waaaa."

Shane studied the older boy's face. The hateful sneer on someone so young was heartbreaking. Shane looked him in the eyes. "What's your name?"

"Frank."

Shane held out his hand. Frank quickly took it and shook hands. "I'm Shane Cartwright."

A gasp was heard around the circle of boys. "The bull rider?"

"Yup, that's me."

"My daddy said that this year you'll probably win your third World Championship in a row."

"That's the plan." He looked into the eyes of Frank, still holding onto his hand. "You know the number one rule of the rodeo?"

The boys shook their heads.

"Good sportsmanship." He glanced around at each of the five boys. "So are you showing good sportsmanship here?"

Frank puffed up his chest. "Of course we are."

Shane let go of Frank's hand and reached out to the little boy they had been picking on. "So, what's your name?"

"Wyatt."

"You're daddy Wyatt Blackman?"

"Yeah, you know him?"

"Sure do. Known him since we were about your age. He's an awesome bull rider. Beat me a lot of times." He ruffled Wyatt's hair. "Tell him I'm going to stop by and see him soon."

"Good thing his daddy ain't here to see his little sissy afraid of sheep."

Shane squeezed Frank's shoulder. "That is enough of that." He looked back at Wyatt. "So tell me, why are you afraid of the sheep?"

"What if I fall off and get hurt like my daddy did?"

Frank started to say something, but the glare from Shane stopped him.

"Your dad was on one of the meanest bulls out there. That's a whole lot different than a sheep." Shane got down on all fours. "Here, get on my back."

"What?"

"Hop on. I'm going to show you, you don't have to be afraid."

Wyatt timidly climbed on. "You holding on?" Wyatt grabbed Shane by the vest and nodded. Shane took off on all fours crawling as fast as he could go. The boys all cheered. Suddenly, Shane spun to the right and Wyatt fell off. Shane reached out for him. "You okay?"

Wyatt was grinning as he picked himself up. "Yeah."

"You see, you fell off and didn't get hurt. That's what riding the sheep will be like. You think you can do it?"

"Yeah."

"Great. I'll be standing here watching." He turned and looked at the other boys. "I hope I never see any of you bullying another kid again."

"We weren't bullying!"

"What do you call it?"

"Just having fun."

"At another kid's expense? That isn't having fun." He looked from one boy to the other. "Everyone is afraid of something."

"Even you?" one of the boys asked.

"Yes, even me. I don't care who you are, something makes you afraid. And I dare say I don't think you would want someone making fun of you for it. Would you?"

They lowered their eyes to the ground, all of them shaking their heads no. "I want you all to apologize to Wyatt. Then I want you to go out there and have fun. Make this the best mutton-busting event ever." He high-fived them all. "Now go get in line."

He watched as the boys ran off together. One of them even matched his steps to Wyatt's so the youngest boy wasn't left behind. Shane couldn't help but smile.

"Shane Cartwright."

He turned at the sound of his name. "Charlene." He grinned as he hugged the petite redhead. "Nice to see you."

"You as well." She laid her hand on his arm. "It's great to see you still playing the hero."

"What?"

She nodded toward the boys. "Wyatt is my son. I was just about to step in when you showed up." A soft giggle escaped her. "Thank goodness."

"I heard you were crazy enough to marry Wyatt." They both laughed.

"He does make things interesting."

"How is he?"

"Doing better."

Shane was watching the boys when Wyatt suddenly did a backflip. Shane chuckled. "Looks like he takes after his dad."

"He sure does." Charlene watched her son laughing with the other boys. "Sort of déjà vu, isn't it?"

Shane looked at her puzzled.

"Don't you remember the first day of kindergarten? The bigger boys were picking on Wyatt Sr. and you stepped in just like you did today and stopped them."

"Aww, I had forgotten about that."

"All the little girls fell in love with you that day."

"Charlene Blackman, are you saying you had a crush on me?" He chuckled.

"Only until Wyatt did his little backflip." She nodded toward the front of the line where Cassidy was pinning numbers on the contestants. "Good thing too, since your heart was already taken."

Shane looked shocked. "I wasn't in love with her in kindergarten. She was only three years old."

"Doesn't mean your heart wasn't already marked by God for her."

Shane sighed.

Charlene hugged him. "I keep praying somehow you two find your way back to where you belong." She kissed him on the cheek. "Nice seeing you."

"You, too. Tell Wyatt I said 'hi'."

"What a beautiful horse."

Cassidy cringed at the sound of Jennifer's voice. She continued to brush Cleopatra. "Thank you."

"Sorry, all that primping is going to go to waste."

"What?"

"You know you can't beat my time. So why push your horse to do something that's impossible?"

Cassidy turned toward Jennifer. The rhinestone shirt and matching hat almost blinded her. Her designer red boots had two-inch heels and her jeans were so tight she wasn't sure how the woman could walk much less ride in them. Was this woman a barrel racer or competing for the most ridiculous riding outfit of the year?

"But at least your horse will look beautiful when she loses."

Cassidy stared speechless at the woman. She couldn't believe she was still talking.

"Of course you could always just not ride. Save face from losing to your ex's new lover. Oh wait, he was never your lover." She fanned herself. "You just don't know what you were missing." Jennifer spun on her heels and strutted away.

"She could give a peacock a run for its money," Allison snickered.

"Can you believe her?"

"Can you believe that outfit? Do you think she can ride in that?" Allison asked. "I'm going to tell my mom to get a picture of her face when the two of us beat her time."

Cassidy giggled. "You know we might not."

Allison stopped brushing her horse and stared at Cassidy. "When was the last time either of us ran over 15.30 anything?"

"You never know."

Allison came around and touched Cassidy's head. "Do you have a fever?"

"Of course not."

"I sure hope you aren't letting her get into your head."

"I'm not." She glanced over her shoulder toward the arena. "Every time I enter the ring, I know all Cleopatra and I can do is our best and we both give it our all. There is no guarantee we will win." She grinned. "But someone needs to tell Divadeville that 13.46 has been the only unbeatable score ever."

"Yeah, but your mom came close."

Cassidy smiled. "Yes, she did." She saddled Cleopatra. "Maybe tonight is the night we come close, huh girl?" Cleopatra whinnied and nodded her head.

Allison laughed. "I hope you do."

Cassidy whispered into Cleopatra's ear, "Let's go beat her."

"I heard that." Allison glanced over at her friend. "Glad to see you got your spirit back."

Cassidy swung up into the saddle. "I never said I wasn't going to try and beat her bad." Suddenly Cassidy stopped. "Oh no!"

"What?"

"I just realized why she wears those awful boots."

"Why?"

"When I was walking Lightning earlier, I noticed he had a tiny round mark on his side. I couldn't figure out how he got it. It was from her heels. She's poking her horse with them." Cassidy covered her face with her hands.

"Do you think Shane knows that?"

"How could he not?" Cassidy felt sick to her stomach. "He is not the man I once knew." She grabbed Allison's hand. "You have to tell her that will hurt Lightning."

"She won't listen to me."

"What do we do?"

"Tonight, nothing. I'll talk with Shane later."

Cassidy and Allison rode together to the holding area to wait for the start of the event. They could hear the announcer talking about the last two events of the night—the barrel racing and bull riding. Cassidy glanced at the far side of the arena. This was the first time in five years she would see Shane ride live.

Allison nudged her. "Focus on your ride, not his."

"I—"

"Then look this way, not over there."

Cassidy felt the blush move up her face.

Allison patted Cassidy's arm. "Now focus. We have a Divadeville to put in her place."

Cassidy took a deep breath then high-fived Allison. "Here's to our best time yet."

Of the eight riders, Jennifer was sixth, Allison was seventh, and Cassidy was last. Just before entering the ring, Jennifer turned and gave Cassidy a smug smile. Her time wasn't as fast as earlier in the day, but good enough to keep her at the top. She flipped her hair as she rode by Allison and Cassidy.

Cassidy wished she could have seen Jennifer's face after Allison's score of 14.76 flashed across the scoreboard. She took a deep breath and patted Cleopatra's neck. "Time to ride the wind."

"Our next rider is Cassidy McDaniel, our winner four years straight. Will she make it five? If she does, she will beat her mother Rachel McDaniel's record for the most consecutive wins here at Berksville Rodeo. This ought to be exciting. We all know the times she put up in the past. If anyone can fly to the top of the leader board it will be her. Cassidy is riding her mare, Cleopatra."

Cassidy leaned over and whispered to her horse, "It's all you, girl. I'm along for the ride."

Cleopatra flew down the tunnel and into the ring, rounding the first barrel with barely an inch between them. She headed to the second barrel, rounding it like it wasn't even there. After flying around the third, Cleopatra opened up and flew from the ring.

The crowd went crazy as the announcer called out her time, "Fourteen seconds flat. We have a new leader."

Cleopatra continued to fly out of the ring and down the tunnel. Cassidy reined her in. No sooner had her feet touched the ground than Miranda, the onside reporter and the cause of Cassidy's nightmares, appeared from nowhere.

"Cassidy, do you have a minute?"

"Sorry, Miranda, I don't. I need to get over to the bull riding."

"I'm heading that way, too. Mind if I tag along?"

Cassidy stopped and glared at her. She knew the woman was just doing her job, but ever since that night she'd caught Shane kissing the blonde Barbie doll, she'd had to endure her. No, she didn't want the reporter to come with her. No, she didn't want to talk to her ever. *NO, NO, NO,* she wanted to scream, but she just kept walking.

"Please."

Cassidy took a deep breath. "Two minutes, I have to take care of Cleopatra and get ready. I'm fourth, so I don't have much time." Especially if she wanted to see Shane ride. And she did.

Chapter 8

Shane rubbed his foot on the back of Torpedo, letting the bull know he was there. The bull tried to kick, but the chute was too narrow. Cautiously, Shane eased down on its back. Torpedo jerked, trying to toss him off, but in the tight pen, he couldn't do it.

"Looks like you're in for a wild ride," Luke said, taking the end of Shane's bull rope to start pulling it tight.

"I heard this one has tossed everyone so far." Shane rubbed the rope, getting the rosin heated and sticky, before putting his hand into the handle of the bull rope. Luke handed him the end of the rope and Shane wrapped it around his hand. He lowered his eyes to the back of the bull's neck, right above his hand, and nodded. The gate swung open.

"*Shane!*" Jennifer screamed.

He jerked his head up at the sound, momentarily losing focus. True to his name, Torpedo flew from the pen. Kicking, the bull bucked forward and spun to the right. It was all Shane could do to hang on. His free hand almost came down, but he quickly adjusted, pulling it back up before it could touch the bull.

Somehow he stayed on. His hat flew off when the bull kicked to his left. He was playing catch-up and the bull knew it. Shane heard the buzzer just before he hit the ground with a bang. He rolled away from the hind legs moments before Torpedo could stomp on him.

The bullfighters quickly moved in. Shane made a dash to the sideline as they herded the bull out of the ring. He grabbed his hat and waved it to the crowd, smiling.

"That wasn't the prettiest ride we've seen tonight, but Shane Cartwright managed to hang on and have the first qualified ride on Torpedo."

The smile left his face the second he saw Jennifer.

"I need to talk to you," she said.

"I can't talk to you right now."

"I need to talk to you." She stomped her foot.

He threw his hands in the air. "I can't deal with you right now." He turned and stormed off.

He had barely gone two steps when Miranda hurried up. He groaned. Of course, she would be looking for him.

"Trouble in paradise?"

For a second, he stared at her. "You know full well why there is no paradise."

Miranda lowered her head. "Sorry."

Her cameraman hurried up. "You found him."

Miranda looked up, smiling. "Shane, do you have a minute for us?"

He plastered a smile on his face. "Of course."

Miranda smiled at the camera. "We are here with hometown cowboy, Shane Cartwright." She gave him her best smile. "It's nice to have you back in town."

"Nice to be back."

"What's it been, five years?"

Shane kept smiling. She knew full well how long it had been. If it wasn't for her... he closed his eyes for a second. He wasn't going there. He just nodded.

"Let's talk about that ride on Torpedo. It looked like he was getting the best of you."

Shane answered her questions on autopilot, smiling and nodding when he was supposed to. All he wanted was to be done with it. Miranda finally nodded at the cameraman and he stopped filming. "I want to interview Tanner next. See if you can find him." The cameraman nodded and strolled off.

Shane inwardly groaned when Miranda stayed.

"Have you seen Cassidy?"

"Of course."

"And?"

"And nothing." Shane kicked the dirt at his feet.

Miranda touched his arm. Shane jerked away. "I'm sorry. I never should have—"

"It happened. No point in talking about it again."

Miranda nodded. "I just wish there was something I could do to fix it."

"You and me both." Shane was done with this conversation, done with women, done with it all. "Listen, I need to get going."

"Are you going to hang around for Cassidy's ride?"

"Definitely."

"It's a shame she doesn't compete on the bulls as much as she used to."

Shane nodded. They both knew the reason for that. Cassidy refused to compete in any rodeo where Shane was. Which was why he had sworn Mr. Scottsdale to secrecy when he signed up. Otherwise, Cassidy would have withdrawn.

Miranda started to reach for his arm again, but dropped her hand. "It was nice seeing you here, Shane. I know the hometown crowd has missed you."

Shane hurried to the stands. For a brief moment, he wondered if Cassidy was still as good as she was five years ago. Of course, she was. What was he thinking? He knew not only was she the best woman bull rider, but if she would compete more, she would easily make it to Vegas.

He climbed the bleachers to the top, old friends greeting him as he went by. A few of them shouted that Cassidy was next. As if he didn't know. The only problem with being from a small town was that everyone knew all of your hopes and dreams. And they all knew that his and Cassidy's dreams of being World Champions—him for overall and her for bull riding—had flown out the window the day he kissed Miranda. Cassidy stopped going to the National Rodeo Championship in Vegas, only competing enough to keep her PRCA card in good standing and in the Professional Women Rodeo Champions.

Shane took a seat beside some teenage boy he didn't know. He could see Jake helping Cassidy prepare for her ride. Women bull riders were a rare breed, and to be as good as Cassidy was even rarer. But why couldn't she be as good as any of the guys in the sport? She had put in the time just like the rest of them, if not more. He smiled to himself. She had been three years old the first time they found her on the practice barrel. Neither he nor Jake had noticed her following them. To this day, they had no idea how she climbed up there. But she had, and there had never been any way to get her off it. She loved riding the bulls almost as much as she did horses.

"Cassidy McDaniel is riding Fireball." Shane groaned.

"Isn't that one of your father's toughest bulls?" Obviously, the boy knew him.

"Yes."

The announcer continued, "Fireball is one of the top bulls this year. Only one person has ridden him and that was Shane Cartwright a few weeks ago in Colorado."

The gate flew open and Fireball shot out of there like the devil himself was riding him. Shane kept his eyes on Cassidy, knowing the bull would kick high to the left before spinning to his right. It was that spin that tossed most riders. Cassidy kept her seat while Fireball twisted and kicked.

Shane didn't realize he wasn't breathing until the buzzer sounded the eight seconds were over. Cassidy jumped from the bull's back and landed on her feet as the bullfighters wrangled the bull out of the ring. She removed her helmet and her long black hair fell across her shoulders and down her back.

She glanced up in the stands right into his eyes. His heart stopped. He tipped his hat. She lowered her eyes and walked away.

Cassidy's heart was racing, and it wasn't from the rush of the bull. How her eyes had known where to look in the crowded stands for him was a mystery she never could understand. She lowered her eyes and dashed to the gate. Would she ever be over him? Her brain said "yes," but her heart betrayed her every time.

Jake came rushing over, picking her up and twirling her around. "Wow, that was a great ride. Do you realize you're on top of the leader board?"

"What?" She turned to look at the board. "But Shane?"

"Shane had a crappy ride. He might have made eight seconds, but the judges scored the bull higher than him. Combined, it wasn't even in the 90s."

"Cassidy." The sound of Miranda's voice pierced right through her. Not again. She turned, putting a smile on her face.

"Do you have a few minutes to talk about that ride?"

They had been friends once, but all that ended when she found Miranda and Shane locked in each other's arms. She took a deep breath. "Sure."

"How did you manage to hang on to Fireball? There were moments I thought he was going to do a handstand."

Cassidy laughed. "There were a few moments I thought the same thing."

"Do you think you have an advantage of riding a Cartwright bull since your families work so closely together and you help train with them at the school?"

Cassidy hated that question, but it came up more times than it didn't. "No advantages. The bulls that come to the rodeo are not the same bulls we teach on at the school. Until today, I haven't seen Fireball, only heard about him." But you knew that, she wanted to shout. Instead, she said, "Knowing a bull or a horse for that matter doesn't give anyone an unfair advantage. If it did, no one would ever be allowed to pick a bull they had ridden before. Every day is a new day and you never know how the bull is going to react."

"Great ride, Cassidy." Tanner patted her back as he strolled by.

Miranda called him back. "Tanner, how does it feel to be knocked out of first by Cassidy?"

"It's not the first time." Tanner winked at Cassidy. "Tomorrow is another day."

Cassidy linked her arm with Tanner's. She smiled at Miranda. "I'm guessing we are done here?"

Miranda nodded to the cameraman. "Yes."

Cassidy led Tanner away. Tanner tipped his hat to her. "Always happy to give you a quick getaway."

Cassidy laughed. "That obvious?"

Tanner winked. "Only to us in the know."

Cassidy reached up and kissed Tanner's cheek. "Thanks for rescuing me."

"My pleasure."

Allison came running up, grabbing Cassidy by the hands. "Wow, just wow. I can't believe that ride. Everyone's talking about it. " She glanced at Tanner and blushed. "You had a great ride too, Tanner."

"Miss Allison, lovely to see you."

Cassidy winked at Allison. "I need to go check on Cleopatra."

Shane stood back watching Cassidy, trying to get the nerve to congratulate her on her awesome ride. He watched her linking arms with Tanner and felt a swell of jealousy. He took a step toward her until a hand on his back stopped him.

"I have been looking everywhere for you," Jennifer said between clenched teeth. "I should have known you would be near her." Jennifer stepped in front of him. She put her finger in his face. "You stay away from her."

Shane pushed her finger away. "You don't tell me what to do." He picked up the pace. Once the door shut behind him he took a deep breath of fresh air and a sigh of relief knowing she wouldn't follow him outside. He was shocked when she grabbed his arm.

"I need to talk to you."

"I can't talk right now."

"Why not?"

"Because I am furious with you. If I say what I want to say, it's not going to be nice."

Jennifer took a step back in shock. "Mad at me, why?"

"Why?" He got in her face. "You nearly got me killed."

"Stop being so dramatic."

He grabbed her by the hand. "Fine. You want to do this now?" He started walking across the parking lot toward his trailer. The long line of cars leaving was not

VICKIE FISHER

making it easy. Car after car was shouting "hi," "welcome back" or just wanted to chat for a minute. He smiled and waved and kept moving.

"Shane, I can't walk that fast."

Shane glanced down at her boots. "That's your fault for wearing three-inch heels to ride."

"Shane, stop."

He turned and glared at her.

"I want to go to the hotel. Let me call an Uber."

"I am not taking an Uber to a place I can clearly see from here."

When he got to the front of the next vehicle in line, he recognized his mother's SUV, and its window was sliding down. "Do you need a ride to the hotel?" Rachel asked from the passenger seat.

"No!"

Jennifer quickly dashed around him, jumping into the SUV.

He glared at her. "We can walk."

"She can't walk all that way in those boots," his mother said, inching the car forward less than a foot.

Jennifer looked at him. "Are you coming?"

He glared at her for another moment before sliding in beside her. He hadn't even shut the door when his mother glanced back and said, "That was not your best ride."

"Someone screamed my name just as the gate opened." He stared at Jennifer.

"I needed to talk to you."

"At that moment?"

"Yes."

Rachel said with a grin, "Did you see Cassidy's ride?"

Jennifer huffed. "I can't believe she's a bull rider."

"And a good one at that," Rachel added.

The car had barely moved an inch with all the cars leaving the rodeo. "We should walk."

"I'm not walking."

He groaned, leaning his head against the back of the seat. Rachel started bragging about Cassidy's barrel race, then glanced at Jennifer. "You had a great ride too, but honey, you need to get rid of those boots. The way you dig them into your horse's sides has to hurt him. Why don't you just wear a pair of spurs? Rodeo spurs have round edges so they don't hurt the horse."

"They're ugly."

"That's why you wear those heels?" Shane's voice rose. "So you can hurt your horse?"

"I'm not hurting him." She glared at Shane. "Don't act like you didn't know. You've watched me ride all season."

Shane groaned. He hadn't watched her. Never in his wildest dreams did he think she would be so cruel to her horse. "Tomorrow, the heels stay in the room. I know you have regular boots. If you want spurs, I will make sure you have a pair. But you will not be hurting your horse again."

"You can't order me around."

"No, but when I go to Mr. Scottsdale and inform him you are abusing your animal, he will disqualify you."

"You wouldn't."

"Not only would I, I will." He pulled out his phone. She slapped it out of his hand. He reached under the front seat for it. "I promise you, if you show up in those boots tomorrow, I will make the call."

"I know you are just having a fit because you don't want the two darlings to lose. But boots or no boots, I will still beat them."

"Not as long as Cassidy's riding Cleopatra," Rachel said. "No one has beaten them in years."

"Humph." Jennifer snorted. "If she's so unbeatable, why is she never in Vegas?"

Both his mother and Rachel turned to look at him. He pulled his hat down over his eyes.

"She always qualifies. She just declines."

"Why would she do that?"

Shane groaned. This bumper to bumper traffic was going to take forever and he was done with this conversation. "She doesn't go because she can't stand to breathe the same air as me." He opened the door and got out. "I'm going to the trailer."

"What?"

"The only thing happening in your room tonight is an argument."

"Why would we argue?"

Shane stared at her in disbelief. "How can you be so clueless?" He slammed the door and stormed away. He could feel Jennifer's glare on his back, but he didn't care. He couldn't take one more second in her presence.

He had never let her self-centeredness get to him before. It wasn't like he was going to spend the rest of his life with her. He knew she didn't love her horse and didn't even care about barrel racing. For the life of him, he couldn't figure out why she wanted to do it. But to think she would harm her horse just so she could win was unthinkable. He was furious more at himself than her, for not realizing the extent she would go to win. He needed to be alone and get his anger under control.

Almost every car he passed, someone put their hand out the window to high-five him, or say "welcome back." A few made a joke about him being beat by a girl. Each time they would add, "but what a girl." And they were so right. By the time he had gotten to the end of the row of cars, his mood was better. That was what living in a small town would do for you.

He checked on the horses, rubbing his hand down Lightning's side. "Sorry boy, I wasn't paying attention. But I promise this won't happen again." He went to the back of his trailer and grabbed the salve out of the first-aid kit. He returned to Lightning. "This will make you feel better tonight. Tomorrow in the daylight I'll get a better look." He stroked the stallion's back. "Unbelievable," he mumbled to himself.

He reattached the roping to the fence and headed toward the bonfire he knew was happening behind the clubhouse. He heard the sweet sound of her laugh before he saw her. She was sitting between Allison and Jake.

Jake looked up and waved him over, scooting closer to Cassidy so Shane would have room beside him.

Shane leaned forward so he could see Cassidy. "Awesome ride tonight."

"Thanks," she said without looking up.

Jake slapped him on the back. "Too bad we can't say the same for yours."

Shane rolled his eyes at his friend. "You can't win them all."

"Hey bud, I think your phone is buzzing."

Shane shrugged.

"Don't you want to see who it is?"

"I know who it is. She's been blowing up my phone for the last ten minutes." Shane stared at the ground. "And no, I'm not answering it."

"Maybe there's hope for you yet."

Chapter 9

Even with two Winnebagos and another horse trailer between them, Shane knew the minute she opened her trailer door and stepped out. He turned over on his back and pretended to high-five God. As long as their strange connection was still there, there was hope. He lay looking up at the ceiling.

He had thought coming back was a big mistake. Now he realized his mistake was twofold—the first was bringing Jennifer with him and the second was not coming home sooner. Cassidy's feelings for him were still there. There were moments he could see it in her eyes.

He rolled out of bed, grabbed his duffle bag from the corner, and swung it onto the mattress. Digging deep into the bottom, he pulled out the red velvet jewelry box and opened it. The rising sun's rays glimmering through the window caught the center diamond, sending a prism of light dancing around the room. He laid back down, staring at Cassidy's ring. The way the tiny diamonds clustered around the larger one reminded him of a rose with diamond leaves. The minute he'd seen it, he knew it belonged on Cassidy's finger. Only he had blown it before he ever got a chance to give it to her. He snapped the lid shut.

He looked around the living quarters of his luxury trailer. Boy, had he gotten ribbed for buying this. Everyone called him the pampered cowboy. He didn't care. Little did they know, this was all for Cassidy. Not that she would have ever needed anything so luxurious, but he wanted it for her. Five years ago, he had spent all his winnings to buy it so he and Cassidy would have a place to live on the road after they got married. It was big enough for six horses and had all the comforts of home. Then he bought the ring. He had been so sure of life. They would win at Vegas, and he would propose right there on the stage for all the world to see. They would get married, have children, and live happily ever after in Grampa's cabin by the lake.

Shane shoved the ring back into its hiding place at the bottom of his duffle bag. Life sure hadn't turned out the way he planned. If this weekend had taught him anything, it was that a memory like Cassidy could not be replaced. He needed to fix the mess he had made of their lives.

The drinking, the women, the devil may care attitude could not drown the memory of Cassidy. He loved her and somehow he had to get her back.

First thing was to get through this last day of the rodeo. Tomorrow he would take Jennifer back to Colorado, break things off with her and give her father two weeks' notice. Then he was coming home. *Cassidy McDaniel, look out. My heart is coming for yours!*

He quickly dressed and headed out the door. He glanced at the makeshift corral. Cassidy was tossing hay to the horses. He started toward her but stopped. No. Allison was right. He had to end things with Jennifer before he even thought to make things right with Cassidy. This weekend, Cassidy had avoided him as much as she could and had barely spoken to him. Today wasn't the day to make things right. Instead, he headed toward the stockyard to help his father and brothers feed the bulls.

Halfway through taking care of the animals, his father asked, "You coming to church with us?"

"What?"

"You know, Sunday morning, praising God," Luke said, slapping him on the back. "Or have you forgotten?"

"No, I haven't forgotten." He punched his brother's arm. "I just didn't think about it being Sunday."

"Well, I hope you are planning on going. It would please your mother to have all her children there for a change."

"I'll think about it."

"You do that. And bring your girlfriend with you." His father tossed the last bull some hay. "Do you both some good."

"We'll see."

Jennifer reached for the phone to read the text message.

Going to church with the family. Breakfast at the Cattleman diner around nine forty-five if you're interested. ~Shane

She sat straight up. Church? Was he insane? She couldn't wait to get out of this backwoods town and back to normal. One more day and she would wipe the dust off from this place and never look back.

She glanced at the bedside clock, eight-thirty. Jennifer groaned. She hated mornings, but today, like it or not, what had to be done couldn't wait. And those goody-two-shoes, going to church, just made things a whole lot easier. She tossed her suitcase on the bed and dug under her clothes for the Ziploc baggy of cherry leaves. She had hoped it wouldn't come to this, but she had to win.

She was in third place behind Cassidy and Allison. Well, she'd show them. Once she gave Lightning an extra dose of Stanazol, he would easily outrun Allison's horse. She smiled smugly. If anyone ever discovered she had been doping her horse, she would play innocent and blame it on Shane. After all, he had promised to make her a winner.

Wouldn't that teach Mr. Perfect a lesson on who to mess with? He thought she didn't see the way he looked at Cassidy or the way he kept sneaking away to watch her compete. Oh no, she had seen it all. No one humiliated her and got away with it. And if he thought for one minute he was going to end it with her, he was crazy. It wasn't over until she said it was. She would destroy him before she let him go.

As for Ms. Perfect, today she and that mare of hers would get what they deserved. Jennifer fingered the bag of cherry leaves. She had to be careful, too many and the horse would die.

Sick or dead, Jennifer didn't care, she just needed Cassidy out of the event. According to Rachel, as long as Cassidy was riding Cleopatra no one could beat her. *Well Miss Perfect, today is your unlucky day. Not only do I have your boyfriend, I'm taking your horse from you, too.* She tossed her head back and laughed. "Winner take all."

She put the bag in her purse, along with the syringe full of Stanazol, and went to take a shower.

The second the preacher said, "Amen," Cassidy flew from the pew and out the door. She stood for a few minutes, taking deep breaths. How dare Shane waltz into church and think it was okay to sit beside her? He could have just as easily sat at the other end of the row next to his parents. But no, he had to sit next to her. And to make it worse, Mr. Triplett had squeezed their shoulders, grinning at them as if they were back together.

Then Shane had the nerve to think he could share her Bible just like they always had. Well, she'd shown him. She dropped it in his lap and refused to look. *Very mature, Cassidy.* She started down the street toward town. She was too mad to wait around for a ride. Maybe by the time she got to the restaurant, she would have cooled off.

She had barely gone a block when Jake honked his horn. "Get in the truck."

She turned, then stopped mid-step. Shane was in the front seat. "No."

Her brother Ben yelled out the back window, "Get in the truck!"

She kept walking.

"You have two seconds to get your butt in this truck on your own or else Shane is going to get out and put you in here," Jake shouted.

She glared at her brothers. She started to say "no" again when Shane opened the door. She quickly ran to the bed of the truck and jumped in.

"You trying to get me a ticket?" Jake jumped out of the driver's seat and ran back to her. "You can't ride back there. It's against the law."

"It's a short ride."

Jake reached over, grabbing her by the arm. "Let's go."

"I'm not riding with him!" Cassidy scooted away from Jake's reach. "If I see Uncle Bob coming, I'll duck."

Luke came around to the back of the truck and jumped in beside her. "I'll make sure she doesn't jump out."

"You do that." Jake shook his head. Before storming back to the driver's seat, he called back to her, "Jesus still loves you even when you act like a brat."

"Shut up." She laid her head on her knees. She knew she was being unreasonable, but they just didn't understand. It hurt too much to be so close to Shane.

There was a battle raging inside of her, one she could only fight from a distance. When Shane was beside her, all she wanted to do was throw her arms around him and never let go. Then the rattlesnake would hiss in her brain, *You'll always be second place to him. He doesn't love you enough.* And the pain became unbearable.

"You want to talk about it?" Luke asked.

"No."

"What are you grinning about?" Shane asked Jake.

He glanced over his shoulder to the back of the truck. "Proof she still loves you."

"How do you figure that?"

"Why else would she be so mad? Anyone else sitting there and she would have been gracious. But you," Jake laughed. "When I wouldn't switch places with her and she slammed her purse between the two of you... it was all I could do not to laugh."

"So, that's why she's mad at you, huh?"

"No, she's mad at me cause I whispered in her ear, 'Is there a problem?'"

Ben leaned up from the back seat. "You know what this means, don't you?"

"What?" they both asked at once.

Ben squeezed Shane's shoulder. "When she's worked up, she rides better. You can kiss any thoughts of winning today out the window."

"Nah." Shane glanced at the clock on the dashboard. "It's not even ten o'clock. There's no way she'll still be mad at five."

Ben leaned back. "We'll see."

Shane glanced to the back of the truck at Cassidy. "Do you really think she still has feelings for me?"

"Yes," both brothers said at the same time.

Shane knew he was grinning like a hyena, but he couldn't help it. She still loved him.

"You can wipe that smile off your face," Jake said pulling into the parking lot of the Cattleman's diner. He nodded toward the hotel. "You have a girlfriend."

"Not for long."

Jake slapped Shane's leg. "I hope you mean that."

"I do."

Ben opened his door. "I'll meet you guys inside. I think Cassidy needs a big brother hug before we go in for breakfast," he said getting out of the truck.

Jake nodded. He glanced back at his sister, "Oh, man." He reached across the seat and grabbed Shane's arm. "You know that saying, 'It's all fun and games until someone gets hurt'?"

"Yeah, what about it?"

"Look at her face. Cassidy isn't mad, she's hurt."

Shane looked at Cassidy talking to Ben. The smile she attempted fell short. Her eyes had lost their sparkle. Shane wanted to run to her, pull her into his arms, and say he was sorry. For what, he didn't know. Somehow he had hurt her again. He hung his head. "I don't understand. All I did was sit beside her."

"I don't get it either." Jake twirled his hat between his hands. "Listen, I know you still love her and she loves you. But you have to stay away from her for now. No more blindsiding her with suddenly appearing or sitting beside her. As long as Jennifer is in your life, my sister is off your radar. Is that understood?"

"The last thing I want to do is hurt her."

"I know that, bro. But you being here, with Jennifer, has done just that."

Shane leaned his head against the back of the seat. "I thought I could do this. Come home, face Cassidy, and prove to her I was over her. The only problem is it backfired. I'm not over her."

"I could have told you that."

"Why didn't you?"

"'Cause you never told me you were coming home."

"Yeah, that was my biggest mistake."

"No, your biggest mistake was kissing Miranda."

Shane groaned. One kiss and his whole world had fallen apart. Somehow he had to make this right. Five years was too long. "I'm leaving tomorrow but I will be back—without Jennifer—and then I'm going to do what I should have done five years ago."

"It's about time." Jake stepped out of the truck. "Now let's go eat."

Shane pulled his phone from his pocket. "You go on in. I have to make a call. Like it or not, I have to see if Jennifer wants to join us."

Chapter 10

She toyed with her pancakes. Every bite was like swallowing cut glass. Cassidy stared at her plate. It wasn't the food, it was her, and she didn't understand why. All he had done was sit beside her. She pushed her plate away. "I'm not hungry. I think I'm going to walk back to the trailer."

"Give me a minute and I'll drive you over," Jake offered.

"No, I need the walk."

Once outside, she took a deep breath, filling not only her lungs but also herself with strength. She knew she was being unreasonable, but she couldn't stop it. It had been bad enough all weekend watching him with Jennifer. And doing her best to keep at least one person between them. But when he'd sat down beside her in church, there had been no escape. He was so close and yet so untouchable. The rattlesnake wrapped around her heart was waiting for it to beat so it could strike and kill her. Shc had slammed her purse between them as if that was enough distance.

She needed to pull herself together and focus on the day ahead, not on the memories of the past. Shane

Cartwright would never again be hers. She grabbed her chest as the snake tightened its grip. She lifted her face toward the sky. *Please give me the strength to get through this day. Please.* She glanced down at the ground. The ache in her heart was suffocating. She bent over, grabbing herself around the waist. *I don't understand why after all this time it still hurts so much.* She wiped a tear from her cheek, took a deep breath, and started walking. *Just one more day. That's all. You can do this.*

She was halfway across the field when she heard the roar of a horse. Something was wrong. A horse didn't roar unless it was badly hurt. She took off running. She reached into her purse and pulled out her cellphone. "Ben, something is wrong with one of the horses."

"Which one?"

"I don't know. I just hear it roaring." She rounded the back of the arena, quickly scanning the makeshift pens of horses. When she saw Cleopatra on the ground, she screamed. Her legs moved faster than they ever had before.

"Cassidy," Ben yelled.

Breathless, she cried into the phone, "It's Cleopatra." She dropped to the ground beside her horse. Antony kept roaring. She ran her hand down Cleopatra's wet neck. "I'm here, girl. I'm here." Antony reached his head over the fence and nuzzled Cassidy's neck. That was when she realized Cleopatra was on the wrong side of the fence. "How did you get out here, girl?"

"Cassidy, Cassidy," Ben kept yelling his sister's name. Cassidy had dropped her phone on the ground and didn't hear him.

Tanner ran up followed by a crowd. He knelt beside her. "Cassidy, what happened?"

"I d-don't..." her voice broke, "know."

Tanner heard a voice shouting from the grass. Looking around he saw the phone and picked it up. "Hello."

"Put Cassidy back on the phone."

Tanner handed the phone to Cassidy. "Ben needs to talk to you."

With shaky hands, Cassidy hit the speaker button. "I'm here."

"What are her symptoms?"

"She's having trouble breathing, flared nostrils, dilated pupils, her heart feels like it's about to jump out of her chest. There's something seriously wrong with her. I can't get her up." She sobbed into the phone, "Please hurry."

"I'll be there in a minute. I'm stopping to get the mobile hospital. It's parked behind the arena."

"Just hurry."

"Keep her calm."

Cassidy tried to get Cleopatra to sit up, but she couldn't budge the mare. The few minutes it took for Ben to get there felt like an eternity. Shane and Jake arrived first. Jake dropped to the ground beside her while Shane quickly calmed Antony down.

"What did you feed her?" Jake asked.

"The same as the other horses—hay and some grain."

"If there was something wrong with either, the other horses would be sick, too." Jake looked around. "She must have eaten something the others didn't." He called out to the crowd. "Hey, look around and see if you can see anything that would have made her sick. If there is poison around, we need to get it cleaned up before all our horses are down." The crowd quickly started searching the ground.

They parted to let Ben through. He did a quick examination. When he drew blood, it looked bright red. "Why is it so bright?" Cassidy's voice trembled.

Ben leaned down and sniffed Cleopatra's breath. "Smells like almond." He called out to those searching the ground, "Be on the lookout for cherry leaves."

Just then, Jennifer ran up with a baggy. "I found this in the trash can over there."

Shane grabbed the bag from her hand. "Cherry leaves. Where did this come from?"

"I told you, in the trash."

Cassidy gasped and grabbed Ben's hand. "Don't let her die."

Ben jumped up. "Jake, come with me." They ran to the back of the mobile hospital. Ben pointed at the IV pole. "Grab that." Ben snatched the sodium nitrate and sodium thiosulfate, along with an IV bag. "Let's go."

Ben dropped down to the ground. "Cassidy, you'll have to be my tech." She nodded. "You need to keep her calm and hold her head still. I have to put a catheter in the jugular vein, so I can start an IV."

Cassidy nodded. She positioned Cleopatra's head on her lap, and soothingly stroked it, whispering words she wasn't sure she believed. "Ben is going to make you better. It's going to be alright."

Ben started the IV, then injected the drugs into the tube. "Let's give the medicine time to work, then we'll get her up and into the mobile hospital. Once I have her stable, I'm going to take her over to the clinic."

"Is she going to be okay?"

"I don't know. Let's just pray we got to her in time." Ben squeezed his sister's hand. "The first hour is the longest. For now, we just pray and wait." He went back to his trailer and returned a few minutes later with a jar of molasses.

"What's that for?"

"Cherry leaves have cyanide. The molasses will bind to the cyanide and help rid it from her system. The quicker we can flush it out of her, the better her chances will be."

"She's having trouble breathing."

"It's labored, but she's holding her own." Ben filled a large syringe with the molasses and forced Cleopatra's mouth open, talking to the horse while he worked. After a few syringes full, he sat down on the ground. "Now we wait."

Cassidy wiped the tears from her face. "Who would do this?" She looked around at the concerned faces of family and friends. None of them would have done this. Then she saw Shane with Jennifer. Was she that hateful?

Ben was right, that first hour dragged by. Each minute felt like a hundred. Sometime during the hour, Shane had brought Antony around to be with them. Cleopatra's ears perked up. It was the first real sign of life she had made. Cassidy laid her head on Cleopatra,

Antony's nose nestled between them. Shane put his hand on Cassidy's back. "She's going to make it."

Without lifting her head, she asked, "How can you be so sure?"

He knelt beside her. "Two reasons. You have the best veterinarian in the state of Wyoming right here," he nodded toward Ben, "and if that wasn't enough," he pointed toward the sky, "...you have God on your side." He rubbed Cleopatra's back. "Hey girl, this is nothing compared to the trouble we first found you two in. He saved you then. He'll save you now."

Cassidy attempted to smile.

Antony stood over her like a sentinel, never moving until they were able to get Cleopatra to sit up. Then he neighed, lowered his head to touch hers, and returned to his rigid stance. Before the hour was up, they were able to get Cleopatra to her feet. It took another fifteen minutes before they were able to get her into the trailer.

Ben secured her with a harness. He turned to Cassidy. "I'll keep you posted."

"I'm going with you."

"Um, no."

"Yes, I am."

Ben grabbed her hands. "There is nothing you can do but wait."

"I can help."

"I have Joelle for that."

"Listen to me." Ben took Cassidy's face in his hands. "This was not an accident. Someone fed those leaves to her. Why?"

"I don't know."

"There can only be one reason. To get you and Cleopatra out of today's events."

"Well, they succeeded."

"No." Ben dropped his hands to her shoulder. "You can't let them beat you."

"I don't have a horse to ride."

"Yes, you do." She turned at Shane's voice. "You can ride Antony."

She shook her head.

"Why not?"

"There is no way I can focus enough."

"So you would rather just sit around and mope for the rest of the day?" Ben asked.

Shane hit the air with his fist. "Someone tried to kill your horse and you're going to reward them by letting them win?" He stared at her. "The Cassidy I once knew never let *hard* keep her from doing what needed to be done."

Her mother entered the trailer. "They're right, you know." Rachel pulled her daughter into her arms. "You not only need to compete today, but you need to win. For Cleopatra." She wiped the tears from Cassidy's face. "Let Ben do his job. Between events, I will drive you to the clinic to check on her. Is that acceptable?"

"She can't stay back here by herself while Ben drives."

"She won't be alone. I'll be back here with her," Ben said.

"Then who's driving?"

Ben tossed the keys to Jake. "He is. I need him to bring the trailer back here in case there's another emergency. Hunter's on-call today, so he can take my place here and I'll take care of our girl."

Cassidy hugged her horse and said a silent prayer. *Please God, place your healing hands upon her.* She kissed her neck. "I'm doing this for you."

Ben led them out of the trailer. "She made the critical first hour." He squeezed Cassidy's hand before shutting the door. "It should be downhill from here."

A wave of fear and anger washed over Cassidy as she watched them drive off.

Rachel put her arm around her daughter's shoulder. "She's in good hands." She glanced at her watch. "Your first event is in less than a half-hour and I think you should ride Misty for that." She glanced at Shane. "I know Antony can do it, but no point in working him when we don't have to."

"But Nancy is riding her in the junior barrel race."

"There's plenty of time between events for Misty to rest."

Cassidy nodded her head. "You're right, Misty for the breakaway event, but Antony for barrel racing." She walked over to Antony, his eyes staring at the back of the trailer. He whinnied when she came near. "She'll be okay, boy." She laid her head on his neck. "She has to."

Cassidy rushed to her trailer to get ready. When she shut the door behind her she collapsed on her knees and prayed as she had never prayed before.

There was a knock on her door. Now what? With dread, she opened it.

Allison stepped up into the trailer. "Your mother told me you would be riding Misty, so I already saddled her for you." She pulled Cassidy into a hug. "Cleopatra will be okay."

"Why would someone do that?"

Allison put her hands on her hips. "So she could win."

Cassidy gasped. "Do you really think it was her?"

"Yes, I do. And so do half the people here." Allison pushed Cassidy toward the bedroom. "You don't have much time. You need to get ready. Today you show her who the real winner is."

Chapter 11

Jennifer did a double-take when she saw Cassidy riding a black horse. No way could Cleopatra recover that quickly. Then she noticed the silver star on the horse's forehead and the silver socks on her feet.

Well, well, well. She had underestimated Ms. Perfect. Who would have thought she cared more about the competition than she did her dying horse? No matter. There was no way that horse could beat a juiced-up Lightning.

Jennifer strutted to the stands. She couldn't wait to see Ms. Perfect lose her first event. The silence in the arena when Cassidy and her horse backed into the corner of the roping box was deafening. Jennifer wanted to scream. Then she realized they must be just as shocked as she had been that Ms. Perfect was still competing.

She relaxed back into her seat until she heard the announcer say Cassidy was riding Misty, the offspring of Cleopatra and Antony. Jennifer almost jumped from her seat. What? Then she smirked. Their horses got more action than the two of them ever had. It was all Jennifer could do to hold the laughter inside.

When Cassidy and Misty flew from the box and that pink lariat went around the calf in 1.89 seconds, putting them at the top of the leader board, Jennifer did jump up and run from the stands. How could this happen? There was no way that horse was faster than Cleopatra. Had she risked everything for nothing?

Jennifer took a few deep breaths. She paced back and forth. No. Impossible. If this horse was faster, then Ms. Perfect would be riding her. A smug smile crossed her face. She had seen this horse already barrel race with some junior girl riding her. There was no way the horse could race twice in one night. Lightning had nothing to worry about.

She stood in the shadow of the stands, listening to the crowd roar as Cassidy received her check for winning the breakaway event. *You might have won this one, but you won't win anymore.*

Jennifer watched as Cassidy rode from the arena. She handed Misty to Allison before going off with her mother. Jennifer followed them as far as the parking lot and watched them get into Rachel's SUV. So she was accepting defeat and leaving. Jennifer smiled.

Barrel racing wasn't for another three hours. She pulled out her phone and called for an Uber. The hotel was the perfect place to avoid Shane. Somehow he knew. She had seen it in his eyes when he grabbed the bag from her hand.

Not only him, but the others seemed to think so, too. She had seen their stares and heard their whispers. They all thought she had done it. She huffed. As if someone of her pedigree would do such a thing. Well, they could think all they wanted. There was no way to prove it.

Cassidy and her mother sat in the waiting room. Ben would occasionally let her go back and see Cleopatra, but never for very long. After an hour, Rachel picked up her phone. "I'm going to call and order us lunch."

"I'm not hungry."

Rachel placed her hand on top of Cassidy's. "You didn't eat much of your breakfast and you have two more events you need your strength for."

"I'm not—"

"You are. And you need food." After calling in the order, she glanced at Cassidy. "God has this. And by competing today you are showing Him you have the faith to believe that."

Cassidy closed her eyes. "I d-do." Her voice cracked. "It's just I feel so sick inside."

"I know you do. Food will help."

Cassidy attempted to smile. "Food's your cure-all."

"Works, doesn't it?" Rachel laughed. "I haven't lost anyone yet."

While her mother was gone, Ben let Cassidy sit with Cleopatra. "She is improving. But I'm not going to lie to you. This is going to be a long recovery."

Cassidy nodded.

"You also need to know she may never be able to compete after this."

Cassidy nodded again. "I don't care. She just needs to live. That's all that matters."

"I'm doing all I can to make that happen."

He half chuckled. "You storming out of breakfast this morning probably saved her life." He put an arm across his sister's shoulder and pulled her to his side. "Otherwise we might not have gotten to her in time."

"Always a silver lining," Cassidy whispered.

"Always," Ben said as the front door chimed someone was there. "That's probably Mom with our lunch." He pointed to the breakroom. "We can eat in there. There's a monitor so we can see to keep an eye on Cleopatra."

"I'll eat here."

"She needs her rest. That means no stimulation from you or anything else. I'm going to turn off the lights and you are coming with me."

It was two-thirty when her mother said, "We need to get you back."

"It's too early."

"Didn't you promise Nancy you would be there to watch her?"

Cassidy sighed. "Yes, but she'll understand why I'm not there."

"Faith, Cassidy," her mother said, and pointed to the door.

Cassidy hugged Cleopatra. "I'll be back. Antony and I are riding for you."

Ben hugged his sister. "Go kick butt."

Rachel pulled up behind the trailer and squeezed her daughter's hand. "Let's go encourage that girl."

"She's really good, you know."

"I do. But does she?"

"No."

"And that is where you come in."

Cassidy quickly found Nancy walking Misty. "You ready for this?" Cassidy asked.

"I'm scared."

"I remember my first big event. My mother practically had to tie me to my horse." Cassidy didn't mention she had been six at the time. She looked around. "It was right here. Of course, it wasn't in the new arena." She pointed to the livestock building. "It was there."

"How did you do?"

Cassidy laughed. "I won."

"I don't know if I can win."

"Then you can't."

Nancy's mouth fell open.

"If you don't believe you can, then Misty won't believe it either and she won't give you the ride you need." Cassidy stroked the mare's neck. "It's not just about you. You and Misty are a team. Do you believe Misty can win?"

"Oh, yes. She's almost as fast as your horse."

"Then, when you start down the tunnel, believe that the two of you as a team will have the best race ever."

Nancy smiled. "Ms. Cassidy, you are the best."

Cassidy joined her mother in the stands to watch the junior barrel racing. Nancy's time of 16.42 was enough to win the junior event. She hurried to congratulate her student.

There wasn't enough time to go back to the clinic, so Cassidy went to get Antony ready. She would need to do some practicing on him to make sure he still understood her commands. She smiled to herself. The last time they had barrel raced together was six years ago when Cleopatra was pregnant with Misty.

When she rounded the back of the trailer, she wasn't surprised to see Shane with Antony. What did surprise her was that her saddle was already on him.

"Hope you don't mind. I got him ready for you."

"Thanks." She rubbed Antony's neck.

"How is she?"

"Holding her own, which is a good thing."

Shane touched Cassidy's arm. "I love her, too."

Cassidy looked into his eyes. "I know you do."

"She's going to be okay."

Cassidy nodded. She turned away from Shane toward Antony. "It's been a long time since we've done this." She smiled. "You think he'll remember?"

"I use him to show my students how to race. So, no, he hasn't forgotten." He nodded toward the livestock building. "I thought it would be better if we practiced out of sight." He glanced at Jennifer's horse. "Billy ought to be here soon to get him ready. I didn't think you'd want to deal with *her.*"

"No, I don't."

"I'm really sorry this happened."

"Me too."

"If I hadn't brought her—"

Cassidy held up her hands to stop him. "Do you have proof she did it?"

"No."

"Then don't say another word. Suspicion does not make it fact." She glanced at the sky. "God knows the truth."

Shane held his hand to her. "Let's get you up on him and let him show you he hasn't forgotten you."

Cassidy ignored Shane's hand, put her foot in the stirrup, and pulled herself up into the saddle. Once seated, she rubbed Antony's neck before nudging him forward into a walk.

When they were safely hidden behind the building, she said, "Let's see what you remember."

She nudged him into a long trot before loping him in both directions. After about fifteen minutes, she started moving him off her legs, making sure he still understood her commands.

She jumped down and hugged Antony. "It's just like old times. You haven't forgotten, have you?"

"Of course he hasn't." Shane patted the rump of his horse. "You trained us both well."

She kissed Antony on the nose. "Now it's time to relax before our big race."

Shane took the reins from her and led Antony over to a bench beneath a shade tree and flopped down in the middle. Cassidy teetered on the edge, as far from him as possible. He silently sighed. For a few minutes, they sat in silence. Then he said, "Why were you so upset this morning?"

She jumped up. "Really, you want to do this now? Have you become so selfish that all you care about is you?"

"No. I just want to talk."

"Talking is for friends." She pointed at herself, then him. "We are not friends." She turned her back to him. "My horse is fighting for her life because someone put more stock in winning than an animal's life." Antony's head jerked away from the grass he was eating and his ears perked up. "That someone believes she can win because she got rid of Cleopatra. And she's right if I don't have my head in the game. You of all people should know that. This is a game of trust. Antony needs to trust me as much as I do him. Otherwise, we need to walk away now. This isn't bull riding where if I'm mad, the bull doesn't care. I get on Antony's back irritated, then he is, too. And whoever did this wins." She put her finger on his chest. "Is that what you want?"

"You know better than that."

"Do I?"

Shane reached out for her.

"Don't touch me." She stepped back from him. "Please go away."

"Cassidy."

"I can't talk to you right now. I need to be alone."

Shane started to walk away. "I'm sorry."

She waved her hand at him. "Please leave."

Cassidy waited until he was gone before dropping to her knees. *Dear Heavenly Father, I know I am being unreasonable. But he makes me so angry inside I just want to scream. I don't know why I can't talk to him about anything beyond horses. Yes, I do. He betrayed me and I can't get past it. Please forgive me. I need to calm my heart, clear my head, and do what I need to do to make it through these last two events. Your word says that no evil formed against me shall prosper. Please, I beg of You, do not let the evil done here today succeed. Your will be done.*

She rose, brushed the grass from her knees, and sat back on the bench. She glanced at her phone—fifteen minutes until showdown. She did not doubt Jennifer was expecting her not to compete; and she wasn't going to show herself until it was time to line up. She was taking no chances that Jennifer had something else up her sleeve.

While sitting around waiting to see Cleopatra, she had plenty of time to Google Jennifer's past wins. What she found was unbelievable. Something had happened to the first and second riders or their horses before each event. One had gotten food poisoning, another diarrhea, a third horse had gotten colic, and the list went on. She couldn't imagine how no one found this suspicious. But no one had gotten gravely ill until today.

Barrel racing had never been about winning for Cassidy. It was about the feeling of freedom, the thrill of flying, and the feeling of two of God's greatest creations being merged into one. But today it was about winning. She couldn't prove it, though she knew in her heart that Jennifer had done this, and Cassidy refused to let her win.

She gently placed her hands on either side of Antony's face and laid her forehead against his. "We are doing this for Cleopatra. You probably feel as horrible about racing today as I do. But if we don't, evil will succeed. We can't let that happen. So, today we run like we have never run before. Together, with God's help, we crush the devil's work. Are you ready for this?" Antony nodded his head and whinnied.

Five minutes before the start time, Cassidy and Antony headed toward the arena. Her family and the Cartwrights were standing there waiting. A sigh of relief escaped her lips. She should have known she wasn't alone in this. Allison rode out to meet her. They held hands as they rode into the lion's den together.

Jennifer had yet to see her. When one of the other women squealed her name, Jennifer spun around in her saddle so fast she almost fell off. The profanity that came from her mouth took everyone by surprise. It took her a minute to realize whose horse Cassidy was riding and the second she recognized Antony, a look of pure hatred crossed her face. For an instant, Cassidy thought she was looking into the face of Satan. Antony immediately took a step back.

Cassidy glanced skyward. *I know You got this.* Her family and friends gathered around her like a wall of protection.

Jennifer jumped down from her horse and ran straight to Shane, yelling obscenities at him. Shane grabbed her by the arms. "Jennifer, calm down."

"Why is she on your horse?"

"She needed a horse."

Jennifer looked over her shoulder and saw everyone staring at her. Like a veil of deception, her face instantly changed to the beautiful façade she hid behind. She smiled at everyone. "How sweet of you to do that," she said sashaying back to her horse. Before mounting him again she glared at Shane. "It's a shame she will make a fool of herself on your horse."

Cassidy smiled at her but didn't say a word. She would let her race answer for them. Today's event was the top eight women. Their times today were all that mattered. Whoever won today won the event. They had drawn numbers to see what place they would run. Allison was third, Jennifer was sixth, and Cassidy as defending champion was last.

Her father and brothers stood guard around Cassidy while Allison's father did the same for her. They were taking no chances of anything else going wrong. Their mothers went to the stands to watch and wait. Cassidy briefly wondered where Luke had gone. He had been there when she first rode up. She barely glanced at Shane, who stood between Allison and Jennifer. The tension was too high for anyone to have a successful ride. Some of the horses were stomping their feet, others neighing.

Luke came running up, carrying a bouquet of roses. He handed each of the women, including Jennifer, one of the flowers. As he handed the roses he gave each of the horses a tiny piece of a peppermint stick.

Willow said, "Luke, you're our hero."

He reached up, took her hand, and kissed it. He bowed. "My lady."

Everyone started laughing and suddenly the tension was broken. Willow tucked the rose into the band of her hat. The others did the same.

Allison's time was 14.13. Jennifer flew through the course in 14.00 seconds, tying Cassidy's best score of the weekend. Jennifer didn't say a word when she rode by Cassidy. She didn't have to. The smirk on her face said it all.

Cassidy sat firmly in the saddle. From her waist, she leaned forward, aligning her body with the line of Antony's neck. She whispered in his ear, "This is for Cleopatra," and they stepped through the doorway and into the long hallway leading to the ring.

Butterflies fluttered in her stomach. Never had a race been as important as this one. Evil would not win today. She glanced heavenward. *Please.* Taking a deep breath she loosened her grip on the reins, gave Antony a nudge, and they were off.

He flew down the tunnel into the arena. Cassidy's heart pounded to the rhythm of the stallion's hooves hitting the ground, *tabdak, tabdak, tabdak.* They took the first barrel with inches to spare, and rounded the second so fast she knew Antony had somehow sprouted wings. Her body felt weightless, she could barely breathe.

Antony's long legs and lean body handled the cloverleaf course with ease. It seemed like only seconds until they rounded the third barrel heading for home. Cassidy's hat sailed into the wind, her braid flapping against her back as if spurring them faster. Antony's mane blew across her hands like feathers in the wind. She was sure they were flying.

It wasn't until they were out of the ring and down the tunnel that she reined him in. Heart pounding, she leaned down and hugged Antony's neck, too breathless to even say wow.

She didn't need to hear the score to know they had won. The roar of the crowd told it all.

Allison rode up beside her. "You did it."

"We beat Jennifer?"

"No."

She felt all the air escape her body. "We didn't?" she barely whispered.

"No, I mean..." Allison was practically jumping in her saddle. "Yes, you beat Jennifer." She grabbed Cassidy's hands. "What I meant was, you broke the record for the best time ever." Allison squealed. "You did it!"

Suddenly, Miranda was throwing a mic in her face. "Cassidy, how does it feel to break the all-time barrel racing record?"

Cassidy looked around at the crowd gathering. "What was our time?"

"You don't know?" Miranda looked at the crowd around them. "She doesn't know her time."

At once the crowd shouted, "13.43!"

Cassidy jumped from Antony's back and threw her arms around his neck. "We did it, boy." She kissed his sweaty neck. "We did it."

Miranda asked a few questions, while they returned to the ring for Cassidy to receive her $45,000 check and belt buckle.

She handed the check to her mother. Her father took Antony. "I'll cool him down. You need to get to the other end of the ring for bull riding."

Her mother hugged her. "Don't know how you can top that, but I know you're going to try."

Cassidy grinned. "You better believe it. This day is all for Cleopatra."

Jake linked his arm in hers and started walking with her. "I wish you could have seen your ride. I don't think Antony's feet even touched the ground. It was like you were flying."

"It felt like it."

"The best part was when it was over. If you could have seen Jennifer's face..."

"I hope I never see her face again."

"That makes two of us.

"I don't understand what Shane sees in her."

Jake squeezed his sister's arm. "She isn't you."

Cassidy rolled her eyes. "Obviously." Halfway to the other side, Cassidy said, "I have to get my gear from the trailer." Jake started toward her trailer with her but she slipped her arm from his. "I'll be okay. I'll meet you over there."

"You sure?"

"I'm sure."

She had barely stepped into her trailer when Jennifer stepped in behind her and grabbed her by her braid. "You think you are so perfect."

Cassidy tried to pull away. "Get out of my trailer."

Jennifer pushed Cassidy's face into the wall, grabbed the buckle from her hand, leaned in, and hissed in Cassidy ear, "This belongs to me."

Cassidy head-butted her. Turning, she snatched the buckle back and hit Jennifer with her shoulder, pushing her away. Jennifer stumbled, falling on the sofa. A long shriek came from her mouth.

Jumping up, she advanced toward Cassidy, a finger pointed at her. "You think he still loves you. Well, he doesn't. He never did." She threw her head back and laughed. A laugh so cold it sent shivers down Cassidy's body. "You think a memory like you can compete with someone like me?" She flipped her hair. "Well it can't." She leaned into Cassidy, her face inches away. Cassidy took a step back. "He told me how your families forced you two together. So the first chance he got, he ran from you. All your memories of him are a lie."

The door flew open and the Sheriff rushed in followed by Shane.

Uncle Bob grabbed Jennifer by the arm.

"Get off of me!" she yelled, flailing to get out of his grip to no avail.

He looked at Cassidy. "Are you alright?"

She nodded. "Just get her out of here."

Bob put his hand on his taser before releasing Jennifer. He pointed to the door. "Out!"

"I'm leaving." She smiled at Cassidy. "Just remember what I said." She waltzed out of the trailer.

"She won't be any more trouble tonight. I'll make sure of that," Uncle Bob said, following Jennifer out the door.

"Cassidy." Shane took a step toward her.

Cassidy pointed to the door. "Leave."

"Cass."

"Get out!"

When the door shut, she paced back and forth for a few minutes. Was it true? Was it all a lie? Was that why he had kissed Miranda, because he had never loved her at all?

The door opened. She spun around, heart pounding, only to see Jake coming in. "What's taking you so long?"

She whispered, "Jennifer."

"I knew I should have come with you." He reached into the corner and grabbed her gear. "You can tell me all about it on the way to the ring."

When Cassidy finished telling Jake what happened, he burst out laughing.

"I'm glad you find this so funny."

"I don't." He tossed her helmet in the air and caught it. "It's just unwittingly, she did you a huge favor."

"How do you figure?"

"Well..." Jake couldn't help from laughing. "I was wondering how after that ride, we were going to get rid of Pollyanna and get the Wicked Witch to show up, and Jennifer did just that."

"What are you talking about?"

He nudged her shoulder with his. "I promise you, Jennifer was planning on getting you so upset that the second you got on that bull, he would throw you off.

Little does she know that, unlike a horse, that bull could care less what kind of mood you're in. He just wants you off. But unknown to her, you ride better mad."

Cassidy stopped mid-stride. "You're calling me the Wicked Witch?"

He laughed harder. "Um, sort of."

She stormed off. Jake grabbed her by the arm. "It's just a metaphor. You could never be the Wicked Witch... maybe her cousin."

"I'm glad you think this is all so funny."

Jake winked at her. "What I think is funny, is how you are going to spoil her plans one more time today." He nudged Cassidy with his shoulder. "What bull did you get?"

"Destroyer."

Jake groaned. "Why do you always get the meanest bulls?" He glanced at her from the corner of his eye. "You picked him, didn't you?"

"Of course."

"Why do you do that?"

"Because I'm as good as any of the guys riding, but I have to prove it over and over again. It doesn't matter how many bulls I ride. Every time, all they see is a girl on a bull. If I get kicked off, no one's disappointed but me, 'cause no one expects me to make the eight seconds. When that buzzer goes off and I'm still on for a split second, it's as if the air has left the building, and you can hear a pin drop, then the audience erupts with surprise. And since half of the points come from the bull, riding the mean ones pushes me to the top."

"You don't have to prove yourself."

"Oh, yes I do." She put on her chaps, took her rope out of her bag, took the braid out of her hair, and finger-combed it before strapping on her helmet. They both climbed up on the chute. She leaned over and patted Destroyer's back, letting him know she was there, before easing down on his back. Jake helped her tighten the bull rope. She rubbed it, getting the rosin warm, before twisting it around her hand. She leaned forward and whispered to the bull, "I know you don't want me on you, but I'm here. Once this chute opens, I'm only on you for another eight seconds. Eight seconds, you can handle that." She sat back up.

"I wish I knew what you always say to them," Jake winked.

"My secret."

Destroyer tried to get her off. Cassidy readjusted, focused her eyes on the back of his neck, and nodded her head. The gate opened and the bull shot out, kicking and twisting to the right. She kept her eyes focused on his neck, her left hand raised and her legs tight against the body of the bull. When he jerked forward, she moved with him. When he twisted to the right she hung on. Destroyer did a half-turn, then quickly spun to his left to knock her off guard. But she knew it was coming and she hung on.

The deafening silence of the crowd right before the buzzer told her she had done it. As the buzzer sounded, the crowd erupted into a roar. She let go and fell to the ground. The bullfighters quickly moved in, getting the bull and her safely away from each other.

She took off her helmet, letting her long black hair flow down her back. She flipped that hair, leaving no doubt she was a woman. Then she glanced at the scoreboard—93 points. She tossed her helmet and high-fived the air. Riding Destroyer had paid off big time. She had done what no one expected.

There were five other riders after her, then she could finally get back to Cleopatra. She hurried over to the winner's box, replacing Tanner who had been the leader.

He shook her hand. "That was one heck of a ride."

"Thanks."

"Next time, I'll get you." He winked. "I would say 'good luck' but that score is going to be hard to beat."

"Maybe. But Shane hasn't ridden yet."

"Ninety-three is one of the best scores of the season." Tanner grabbed his gear and left.

She watched the next two riders get bucked off, then it was Shane's turn. He had chosen Diablo, a bull as mean as Destroyer with the ability to score high. When the gate opened, the bull hit it with its hind legs, spinning him back into the chute, causing Shane to have a re-ride. The bull for the re-ride was Fireball, the one Cassidy had ridden on Friday. The last time Shane had ridden him he had scored a 94, the best of the season. All Cassidy could do was watch and wait.

Shane had his best ride of the weekend. And the crowd waited breathlessly for his score to be flashed. When it was announced as 92, there was a slight moment of shock as they realized that Shane, the top bull rider in the circuit, had come in second behind Cassidy.

She sighed in relief, not that she had won, but that this weekend was finally over. All she had to do now was head over to the winner's circle. Then she would be finished and could get back to Cleopatra.

Chapter 12

She knew Shane was there before he even said her name. Taking a deep breath, she continued to load Misty on the trailer, ignoring him.

"Cassidy, I'm not here to talk to you."

She took a deep breath. "Then why are you here, Shane?" She looked up and saw that Antony was with him.

"I want you to keep Antony until I get back."

"Get back?"

"I'm heading to Colorado in the morning. There are things I have to finish up there and then I'll be back." He patted his horse. "Until then, I think it would be best for Cleopatra if he was here with her. Thanks to Ben, she's going to pull through, but we both know that Antony will give her the strength and willpower to heal quicker."

Cassidy turned her back. She didn't want Shane to see the tears welling in her eyes. Her voice choked up when she said, "Thank you."

He led Antony into the trailer. "I plan on being back before the weekend. But if I'm not, would you bring him to the next rodeo?"

"I'm not—"

He put his hand up. "If this weekend proved anything, it's that we can be in the same space and the world won't end. There is no reason for you to avoid me any longer. If not friends, we can still be competitors. After all, you owe me."

"Owe you what?"

"The chance to beat you." He grinned. "Anyway, it's time the rest of the circuit knows who the real person to beat is."

She tried not to smile, but she couldn't help it. "Maybe."

When Shane turned to walk out of the trailer, he patted Antony's rear. "Take care of our girls." Then he was gone.

Cassidy watched until he was out of sight, then slid down the wall of the trailer, legs barely managing to support her. She laid her head on her knees. The whirlwind of emotions had her mind in a jumbled mess. Jennifer's words kept playing over and over in her head, but Shane's actions screamed a different story.

Tears flowed down Cassidy's face. It took a few minutes before she was able to pull herself together. She patted Misty. "I'll take you home." Rubbing her hand down Antony's back as she walked by she added, "Then we go see Cleopatra."

Ben opened the back door of the clinic for her. "I've been expecting..." He stopped when he saw Antony. "You can't bring him in here!"

Cassidy ignored her brother and kept walking through the doorway.

"Cassidy," he said.

She stopped and stared at him. "Antony being here is the best medicine for Cleopatra."

"Isn't that why you're here?"

"We both are."

"The room isn't big enough for two horses."

Cassidy opened the door to the equine recovery room. Cleopatra was suspended from an overhead hoist connected to the ceiling, keeping her upright. The walls were padded but the padding for the floor was folded off to the side. It wasn't needed. There was a chair beside her, probably where Ben had been sitting. The room was bigger than two stalls put together and was more than enough room.

The second they entered, Cleopatra lifted her head. A soft neigh barely left her mouth. It was the first real sound she had made all day.

"Alright, but only for a little while."

"We're staying the night."

Ben rolled his eyes. "Fine, but you're cleaning up after him."

"Of course." She handed Ben a bag of food. "Mom made us dinner." She gently stroked Cleopatra's neck, making sure not to touch the IV. Antony stood in front of her, rubbing his head against Cleopatra on the opposite side.

"She looks better."

"She's improving, but not out of the woods yet."

"How long does she need the IV?"

"Until her urine runs clean." Ben nodded toward the tub a catheter drained into. "It still has a lot of red in it. And until that's gone I have to keep flushing her system."

A few hours later Ben said, "You need to go home. There's nothing you can do here."

"Cleopatra needs us."

"Then you can sleep on the sofa in the waiting room."

She got up and went over to Antony, pulling her sleeping bag off his back. "I'm sleeping right here."

"Fine." Ben got up. "I'm going to get some sleep then. I would advise you to do the same."

She nodded and laid her sleeping bag on the floor in front of Cleopatra. She didn't worry about harnessing Antony. She knew he wouldn't move from Cleopatra's side.

Ben turned off the lights and locked the back door. But before going to his office he said, "I have an app on my phone that lets me know if her vitals change. So if she needs me, I'll know." He winked at Cassidy. "Lucky for me there's no sound, so I won't hear you snoring."

"I don't snore."

"Let's not find out." He grinned and shut the door.

Cassidy tried to close her eyes, but her mind was going a thousand miles a minute. She sat up and leaned against the padded wall. "Remember when Shane and I first found you? I was ten and he was twelve. We were out riding when we saw the two of you had crashed through the frozen lake. We thought Antony was supporting you, but when I crawled out on the ice and put the lasso around you, and Shane started to pull you out, Antony sank beneath the water. Seems like you were both supporting each other."

"And you were crazy enough to jump in the freezing water to rescue him."

Cassidy squealed at Shane's voice. It took a few seconds for her to calm her heart. "What are you doing here?"

"Same as you. No way could I sleep. So, just like that night so many years ago, we sit here and wait. Only this time, it's Cleopatra, and not both of them we're praying for." He laid his forehead against Cleopatra's for a moment before petting Antony. Then he sat down, leaning on the opposite wall from her.

He didn't say another word. He didn't have to. She knew he was there for her as much as he was for Cleopatra.

It wasn't long before she fell asleep. In the morning, she woke and he was gone.

"He left an hour ago," Ben said as he checked Cleopatra. "Almost twenty-four hours... her vitals are much better and her urine is almost clear. Another bag of fluids and we should be able to stop the IV." He checked her legs. "She's still too weak to stand on her own, but it won't be long."

Chapter 13

What was taking him so long? Jennifer dragged her vanity chair to the bedroom window. She was tired of standing and watching for him. She glanced at her diamond-studded watch. Shane should have been here by now. Had he decided to stay in Wyoming? She paced the room. He wouldn't, would he? No way. For one, he had to bring back her horse and two... she hissed. No way would he have chosen the boring girl over someone as exciting as her. He was just running late, that was all. Once he returned, they would fix this little misunderstanding. She pulled her shirt open a little further. No way would he be able to resist.

She growled. The whole trip had been a disaster. The minute they had driven into Wyoming she felt a shift in him. And once they got to his parents' house, he had totally shut her out. Lastly, she couldn't believe it when he told her they were done, put her in the rental car with Billy, and sent them on their way to the airport. She had been livid. How dare he pack her off like someone's unwanted luggage? She had the short flight and all of last night and today to figure out how to get her plans back on track.

They were *not* done. He just had to get away from *her*. Then they could make things right. Who would have known that memories could have such a stronghold on a man? And that was all Cassidy McDaniel was... a memory, nothing more.

Strutting by the mirror, Jennifer admired her reflection. She fluffed her hair and retouched her red lipstick. Her black lace bra peeped out from the half-opened shirt she had tied at the waist. Her diamond teardrop necklace stopped at her cleavage. This was the outfit she had worn the first night she seduced him. She smiled. *Shane Cartwright, there is no getting away from me.*

Jennifer must have been watching for him because before Shane could get Lightning out of the trailer, she came rushing over, throwing her arms around him, almost knocking him off balance.

"Whoa." He took her arms and untangled himself from her. "What are you doing?"

"I missed you." She tried cuddling up to him. He turned his back to her. "Didn't you miss me?" She pouted.

"Have you forgotten we broke up?"

She ran her fingers gently down his arm. "You didn't mean that."

He started to turn back to the horse. "I most certainly did."

She toyed with the teardrop necklace. He couldn't help but follow her hand. When he saw the open shirt and the lacy bra, he knew what she had in mind.

"But you love me."

Shane froze. The word raked through his body like nails on a chalkboard. He spun to face her. "This," he pointed from her to him, "has nothing to do with love."

Her hand flew to her chest. "I love you." She took a step toward him. He backed away.

"No, Jennifer, you don't."

"I do."

"Then, I'm sorry, but I could never love you."

She laid her hands on his chest. "But why?"

He looked into her emerald eyes and saw only emptiness. Unlike Cassidy, whose eyes were full of warmth and love. He removed her hands from him. "There is only one woman I have ever loved. And if I'm honest with myself, I will never stop loving her. And that is Cassidy."

Jennifer slapped him. Shane grabbed her hand. "Get out of this trailer, now." Turning, he took Lightning by the rein and started out of the trailer.

"What are you doing?" She grabbed his arm, stopping him.

"What does it look like I'm doing? I'm putting your horse in the pasture. Then, I'm going in and giving your father my two weeks' notice."

"You're what?" The screech of her voice grated on his nerves. How had he never noticed that before?

"You heard me."

He removed her hand from his arm and once again headed out of the trailer. She grabbed the back of his shirt with both hands, pulling him backward. He lost balance and fell, hitting the floor almost beneath Lightning's feet. The horse neighed and sidestepped away. Before Shane had a chance to get up, Jennifer started kicking.

Backing away from her, he managed to stand up. "Jennifer, get a grip."

So intent was he on avoiding her two-inch heels, he didn't notice her throwing herself at him, kicking and clawing. She screamed, "I hate you!"

He grabbed her by the shoulders, holding her at arm's length. "Jennifer, if you think this behavior will make me change my mind, you are mistaken."

"No one breaks up with me." She tried to kick him but was too far out of reach. "No one."

"Better now than when you go to jail."

"I'm not going to jail."

"What you did to Cleopatra could very well land you there." Shane glared at her. "The penalty for animal cruelty is one to five years."

"Prove it."

"I'm not the one investigating it and all the other sudden illnesses of riders and their horses this past year."

Jennifer gasped. For a moment her shoulders seemed to cave in on herself. Then, like a flash, her face contoured into an evil sneer. "You will pay for this."

"The only thing I have done is make the mistake of wasting almost a year of my life with you. That's punishment enough."

She yanked herself from his hands. When she reached the door, she abruptly veered to the far side of her horse and dashed to the front of the trailer. She stooped down and started tossing things to the floor from the locker where he kept the first-aid kit for the horses.

"Stop it." He dodged the box of gloves she threw. Reaching down, he grabbed her by the waist trying to pick her up. But she was like a madwoman and fought him. "There's nothing of yours in there."

"You're right, it's not mine." She pulled out a bottle he had never seen before. "It's yours."

"What is that?"

"As if you don't know." She sneered at him. "I'm going to let everyone know that the great Shane Cartwright dopes his horses."

"That's a lie." He reached to grab the bottle, but she pushed all her body weight into him, knocking him off balance and into the wall of the stalls. It was all the time she needed to jump up and bolt from the trailer.

Billy came around the side. "I'll take care of Lightning. You take care of her."

Shane nodded and took off running. He caught her just as she entered her father's study. Garrett glanced up in surprise as the two of them stormed in. "What's going on here?"

Jennifer leered at Shane before handing the bottle of Stanazol to her father. "Daddy, it breaks my heart to tell you this, but..." she lowered her head and pretended to wipe tears from her face. "...I found out this weekend that Shane has been doping my horse."

"That's not true," Shane countered.

"Then explain how that got in your trailer," she accused.

Garrett looked from the drug to Shane, a stunned look on his face.

"Sir, I assure you I have never seen that bottle before."

"And I assure you it's his!"

Garrett glanced from the bottle to Shane again. "This is unbelievable."

Jennifer smiled sweetly at her father. "Daddy, you know I would never lie to you."

He lowered his head, staring at the bottle, then back at Shane. "Never would I have imagined—"

"Sorry to interrupt, sir," They all turned as Billy entered the room. "I have proof the Stanazol belongs to your daughter."

"You're a liar." Jennifer pointed a finger at Billy. "He probably gave it to Shane." She stomped her foot. "I want both of them fired, now."

Billy handed a flash drive to Garrett. "The proof is on here."

Jennifer went to snatch the drive from her father, but he curled his hand around it. "Let's see what we have here." He put it in his laptop and started to watch. "Jennifer!"

He flipped the computer monitor around so she could see. There she was injecting something into her horse. "That proves nothing. It could have been anything."

"Sir, if you continue to watch, you will see that after the race I checked her saddlebag and you can clearly see the bottle in there. Continue watching and you will see this was not a one-time thing."

"You put it in there," Jennifer accused.

"Why would I do that?"

"So, I would win."

"What do I care if you win or not?"

Jennifer put her hands on her hips. "To keep your job."

Billy shook his head. "Helping you is not my only job here."

She grabbed him by the arm, turning him toward her. She leaned into his face. "What gave you the right to spy on me?"

"Your father hired me to not only help you but to watch out for you. I was only doing my job."

Garrett was speechless as he continued to watch the video. Time after time, his daughter was injecting her horse. He stared at Jennifer.

"I didn't know what I was doing. He," she pointed at Shane, "told me to do it."

"That is not true."

Garrett looked at Shane, then Billy, and finally Jennifer. He ran his hand over his forehead before pulling the flash drive from the computer. "Billy, thank you for clearing this up. You are dismissed."

"Yes, sir." Billy nodded his head at Shane. At the door, he turned. "Oh, by the way, that is not my only copy. And if I ever hear that Shane or anyone in his family has been falsely accused of doping, that video will go out to every nook and cranny of the internet, and it will be your name that is destroyed."

"Is that a threat?"

"No, sir. A promise. Just wanted to let you know in case someone's malicious intent was to destroy a good name." He looked at Jennifer. "I'll go pack my stuff and be out of here before dinner."

Garrett looked at his daughter in disgust as he pointed to a chair in front of his desk. "Sit down and don't move a muscle. I will deal with you in a minute." He looked at Shane. "I have dealt with your family for years and I know their character, which is why I hired you. I assure you this will not leave this room." He stared at his daughter. "I would hate for your family's good name to be tainted by a lie."

"Thank you, sir."

"I will be sorry to see you go."

Shane glared at Jennifer. "There is something else you need to know."

"Shut up!" Jennifer jumped from her chair, throwing herself at Shane.

Shane blocked her hand before she could smack him.

Garrett grabbed his daughter by the waist. "Sit down," he ordered. He stood behind her, both of his hands firmly on her shoulders. He glanced at Shane. "You were saying?"

"Something you need to know. This weekend, Cassidy McDaniel's horse was fed cherry leaves." He scowled at Jennifer. "I have heard people talking and they think it was Jennifer."

"Prove it."

"If I could, I would."

"Is there an investigation?"

"Yes, sir, there is." He refused to look at Jennifer. "And not just this weekend. There have been a lot of sudden illnesses of other barrel racers and their horses, at events where your daughter has competed. They are looking into them also."

"Coincidence or something else?"

"That's what they're looking into."

"What a mess." Garrett dug his hands into Jennifer's shoulders.

"Ouch." Jennifer squirmed, trying to get out of her father's grip.

"I'm sorry this has happened. Have no fear, I will take care of it." Garrett reached out to shake Shane's hand. "I'm also sorry we're parting on such terms."

"So am I." Shane felt like he was shaking the dust of the devil off his back as he hurried out of the house. If he had left anything in Jennifer's room, she could throw it away. He didn't want it. He went to his apartment over the stables and packed his stuff. He had left home five years ago and all he had was a suitcase and one small box of stuff to prove it.

Before leaving this property, he needed to search his trailer. Make sure nothing else was hidden. Then find Billy. He tore apart every inch of the trailer, emptying every locker, and moving anything that could be moved to look behind it. He tossed everything on the floor without worrying about putting it back. He had plenty of time to do that once he got home. *Home*, his heart filled with relief. He was heading home.

Moving into the living quarters, he did the same thing. He even pulled the sheets off the bed and took the pillows out of their cases. He was leaving nothing to chance. He looked around at the mess. Good thing he didn't have much.

There was a knock on the door. Shane opened it to find Billy. "I was just coming to look for you."

Billy looked around. "What a mess."

"Not leaving anything to chance."

"Can't say I blame you."

"I'll clean it up when I get home. I don't want to waste another second here."

Billy held out his hand. "Just wanted to say good-bye before I hit the road."

Shane took his hand, then pulled him in for a bro hug. "Listen man, I have to thank you for what you did. This could have turned out really bad."

"Unfortunately, I know firsthand how it could have been."

Shane took a step back. "What do you mean?"

"A few years back, something similar happened to someone close to me. He lost everything—his wife, his kids, his good name, his ranch—and there was nothing I could do to stop it. By the time they proved he was innocent, the damage was already done. Half the people to this day still think he was guilty." Billy wiped his eyes with the back of his hand. "The first time I saw Jennifer doping her horse, something snapped inside and I had to record it. I couldn't help my friend, but maybe I could help someone else if necessary."

"I'm glad you did." Shane bent down and picked up the cushion for the sofa. "Can I ask why you didn't stop her?"

"It was her horse and as long as she wasn't hurting someone else's," he looked down at the floor, "I'm sorry to say, I didn't care." He picked at a cuticle. "Can't say I've cared about much of anything the last few years."

Shane squeezed his shoulder. "Maybe it's time to start again." Billy nodded and backed toward the door. Shane added, "I'll be praying for you."

"Thanks. It sure won't hurt."

Shane followed him out, checking to make sure all the doors of the trailer were locked. "Where you headed off to?"

"Thinking about going back home to Oklahoma. You?"

"My heart never left Wyoming, so I'm going to get it back."

They shook hands one last time. "Good luck."

Shane backed his trailer around and headed toward home. Without a horse, he could drive a little faster. When his rear wheels crossed the state line from Colorado into Wyoming, he rolled down the window, filled his lungs with good old Wyoming air, and started singing the state song. The words washed over him, filling his soul with a joy he hadn't felt in a long time.

Suddenly, he was giddy with laughter. Once again, he had turned into his father. Didn't matter what the weather was like or where they had been, the second the back wheels crossed into Wyoming, his window came down and his father started singing at the top of his lungs. Then they would all join in. No one cared if they sang off-key. It had just been fun.

Shane looked in his rearview mirror, half expecting to see the McDaniel trailer behind him. For as long as he could remember the two families had ridden the circuit together. Their parents had competed in the early years, before focusing solely on being rodeo contractors. No matter what, they dragged their families with them.

The life of a rodeo brat had been fun and the convoy coming home had always been the highlight of the weekend for Shane. Especially when his father's trailer was first in line. The deal was whichever family won the most money got to lead the way home. When he was little, the convoy of their personal trailers and the stock trailers always excited him. It had been a long time since he felt the thrill of belonging to a parade of family, friends, bulls, and horses. It had been too long. It was time to get his life back on track.

He rubbed the back of his neck. The lack of sleep and the stress of the last weekend was starting to wear on him. Up ahead he saw the neon lights of the diner his father always stopped at. He pulled to the back of the lot. Food first, sleep second.

After eating the best fried chicken dinner, he opened the door to the trailer and groaned. He had forgotten the mess he left. He made a path to the bedroom by pushing the stuff to the side with his foot. He was too tired to deal with it now. He flipped the mattress back on the bed, grabbed a pillow from the floor, then laid his sleeping bag on the bed and crawled in. Little sleep and too much driving had him exhausted. His head barely touched the pillow when he was out.

"Shane, I need your help." Miranda came around the corner of the trailers.

"What is it?"

She twirled her long blonde hair around her finger. "I don't know how to ask this."

"Just ask." Shane started to open the door to his trailer.

"I caught Doug kissing another woman."

He spun around. "What?"

She looked near tears. What should he do, hug her? No, wouldn't that be like cheating on Cassidy?

"Kiss me." Miranda said.

"What? No!" He took a step back.

"You have to."

"No, I can't."

She hurried to the back of the trailer, then rushed to him again. "Hurry, he's coming."

"Who?"

"Doug. I have to make him jealous." She started to take a step toward him.

Shane put his hand out. "No."

"You're the only one I can trust to not make this something it's not. It's not like it's a real kiss, It's just for show, nothing else."

"I can't do that to Cassidy."

"She's not even here. She'll never know."

"I'll know, and God will know."

Miranda rushed back to look to see how close Doug was.

"Please, Shane. It's the only way I can make him pay."

Everything inside of Shane screamed not to do it, but it was just a kiss, not really cheating, just a favor for a friend. Cassidy would understand. "Alright."

She waited until Doug was almost to them before running back and throwing her arms around him, knocking him into the trailer. Her lips touched his. He started to push Miranda away. This was wrong. Then the air was filled with the worst sound he had ever heard—the scream of someone dying. He looked up to see Cassidy at the other end of the trailer. The sound was coming from her. One look at her pale face and eyes filled with agony and his world collapsed around him.

Before he could call out to her, she was gone. His heart dropped to his stomach. He pushed Miranda away and ran toward Cassidy, but he didn't know where she had parked her trailer. He ran from row to row, calling her name, panic bubbling up inside of him. He had to find her.

"Cassidy." His heart filled with relief. There she was. He ran as fast as he could but she was already pulling away.

Please, God, let me catch her. *He grabbed the door handle but it was locked. He banged on the door, but she refused to stop.*

She turned, tears streaming down her face. "I hate you." Then, she floored her truck and was gone.

He woke in a sweat, his heart pounding. Shane put an arm over his head. It had been a long time since he'd had that nightmare. He sat up and grabbed his phone. Five A.M. He took some deep breaths, trying to calm his racing heart. He reached down and lifted his duffle bag onto the bed. By the light of his phone, he pulled Cassidy's picture from the inside pocket where he had it hidden. He rubbed his finger across her face. *Somehow I'll show you how sorry I am, and that my love for you has never wavered even when it might have seemed like it to you. You can trust me, Cassidy, and I'm coming home to prove it.*

He quickly dressed and went to the restaurant to eat breakfast. Halfway through, he realized he had left his thermos in the trailer. He groaned. Who knew where he had tossed it? Guess one large coffee would have to do until he stopped for gas later and a quick lunch. If he made good time, he ought to be home by early afternoon. *Home.* He was going home. He couldn't keep the smile off his face.

He was just about finished eating when an extra-large travel mug flopped down on the table in front of him. "Bless my soul, I thought my eyes were deceiving me."

He glanced up in surprise at the gray-haired waitress. He grinned. Molly had been waiting on them since he was a little boy. "You're still working here, I see."

"Thought you might be needing this for the long ride home."

"You remember me?"

The woman put her hands on her hips. "Shane Cartwright, I might be an old woman, but I never forget a handsome face." She took the seat across from him. "I'm assuming that since you're back in this wonderful state of Wyoming that you are finally heading home."

"You assumed right."

She grinned. "Nothing will make your momma happier than to have her prodigal son come home."

"Don't know about being the prodigal son, but I know she'll be happy."

The bell rang when someone entered. Molly pushed herself up from his table. "Break time's over. You be safe driving, you hear."

"Yes, ma'am."

"And when you get home, patch things up with that pretty girl of yours. I miss her, too."

Shane tipped his hat. "That's the plan."

Molly's face brightened. "I love a happy ending."

Chapter 14

Cassidy was standing on the bottom board leaning on the fence, looking at Ben walk Cleopatra around the paddock. Antony stood by watching.

"She's going to be weak for a little bit, so no running or no riding, nothing but relaxing." Ben looked at Cassidy. "If this was anyone else's horse she would still be at the clinic."

Cassidy nodded. She felt him coming up behind her, even before Antony perked his ears up and whinnied. She was afraid to turn to see if Jennifer was with him. Had they kissed and made up and now he was back for his horse? She felt the anger bubbling inside of her. How dare he bring her here?

Without warning, Antony's nose was in her chest, pushing her off the fence, and she was falling right into Shane's strong arms. She looked up into his rich brown eyes, felt the warmth of his arms envelop her, and for a second, her heart shouted with joy. Another beat and the rattler struck. *Cheater,* it shouted, bringing her to her senses. She struggled to get out of his arms. "Let go of me."

Shane was grinning. "Hello, Cassidy."

"Don't talk to me." She spun on Antony, pointing her finger at him. "Why did you do that? No treat for you." She stormed into the paddock and into the barn. Ben's laugh followed her, making her angrier. How dare her heart betray her like that? She grabbed a pitchfork and started toward the first stall.

"Cassidy."

"Get your horse and go."

"I'm not here for Antony."

She stabbed the fork into the dirty hay, tossing it into a nearby wheelbarrow. "Then why are you here?"

"I want to talk to you." His fingers brushed her hand before he took the pitchfork from her.

"I don't want to talk to you." She grabbed the pitchfork back. "I have work to do. Go talk to your girlfriend."

"I don't have a girlfriend."

For a second, her heart tried to control her actions, but her brain was smarter and stepped in. "Then, go talk to Ben or Jake. There's no one here who wants to talk to you."

"*Mon coeur.*"

Her heart filled with love at the familiar words, before the truth pierced it with suffocating pain. "Your heart." She stabbed the pitchfork into the hay. "How dare you call me that?" She pointed to the door. "Get out." When he didn't move, she shrieked, "Get out!"

"Fine." He slowly backed away with his hands in the air. "But we will be talking."

She could still hear his voice, but not what he was saying as he spoke to Ben. How dare he think he could waltz back in and start using his nickname for her? *Mon coeur.* Ever since he had learned it in French class, he had been calling her that... my heart. And now the words that once filled her with love coiled around like a rattlesnake ready to strike.

She had finished the first stall and was starting on the second when Ben stormed in. "I don't get you one little bit."

She kept cleaning without looking up.

"Cassidy." He snatched the pitchfork away from her.

She put her hands on her hips. "What is it with everyone trying to stop me from doing my job?"

"Your job?"

Cassidy kicked some dirty hay. "Yeah."

"So, what... did Dad fire Mason?"

"Of course not."

Ben put the pitchfork back on the rack. "Then, it's his job you're doing."

"Whatever."

"What's your problem?"

"I don't have a problem."

"Really." He lifted his sister's face to look at him. "I don't understand how you can pray for something to happen and when he finally shows up, you won't even talk to him."

"I just can't deal with him right now."

"If not now, then when?"

She shrugged.

"I know what he did was wrong." Ben gave her a half hug. "But five years is too long to be carrying that hurt around."

"Hurt!" she yelled. "Hurt doesn't even come close. He deceived me, my heart, my dreams, my everything. With one stupid kiss, he showed me my whole life was a lie. Talk to him? *No.* I don't want to talk to him. Not now, not ever." She stormed out of the barn, ran into the house, and up the stairs, slamming the door to her bedroom and throwing herself on the bed.

The tears poured out. Cassidy knew she was being irrational, but she couldn't help it. Every time she looked at him, she saw him taking Miranda into his arms and kissing her. Five years and the memory burned a hole in her heart just as intense as it had that night. No. She couldn't forgive him. His betrayal ran too deep.

She sobbed into her pillow. She didn't hear her mother come in until she felt a hand on her back and then felt the mattress sink beside her. Her mother just sat there rubbing her back. When the sobs slowed down, she handed Cassidy a tissue. "Want to talk about it?"

Cassidy shook her head.

"I talked to Ann today... she said that he's home to stay."

"He's not leaving?"

"Only to do the rodeos, but he'll be back every Sunday or Monday."

Cassidy groaned.

"There's no running from him anymore."

She wiped her eyes and sat up. "I wasn't the one who ran away."

"No, but we all know he left because you refused to talk to him."

"He lied to me."

"How did he lie?"

"He said he loved me."

"That was never a lie. He loves you just like you still love him."

"Doesn't matter. I can't trust him. Love without trust is worthless."

"Somehow you will have to find a way to forgive him."

"Never."

"Then I feel sorry for both of you."

"Both of us? It's his fault."

"Yes, he hurt you, but for the past five years it's been all you, making sure the pain kept festering. Not him."

"He never came home."

"He is now." Her mother hugged her before getting up. "What are you going to do about it?" Cassidy watched as her mother softly closed the door behind her. The words echoed in her head. *What are you going to do about it?*

She laid down, staring at the ceiling. *Nothing, absolutely nothing.* There was no denying her heart wanted him. It always had, but she couldn't trust him. She had never kissed another boy, never even went on a date with anyone but Shane. Yet he had flipped from one woman to another until he ended up with the devil herself. If blonde bimbos were his type, it didn't matter what Cassidy's heart wanted. He would grow tired of her again and move on.

No, she couldn't take that risk. She put her hand over her heart. She could barely feel it beating, unlike when it was broken and she could hear it hammering in her head. A barely beating heart was easier to live with than a broken one.

Chapter 15

She pushed the roping dummy to the center of the floor and checked her phone for the third time. Still no text from Allison. Where was she? She was never late. The door flew open and Timmy came running in.

"Slow down," his mother, Janet, yelled after him. "One of these days he just might enter a room like a sane person."

Cassidy laughed. "Then, how would we know he's here?"

"Ms. Cassidy, where's Ms. Allison?"

"She must be running late."

The other students slowly arrived and she looked around at the small group of boys and girls. "Guess it's just you and me tonight."

"Mr. Shane." Wyatt jumped up and ran across the room.

"Hi, Wyatt." He ruffled the boy's hair. "I didn't realize you were in this class."

Cassidy stood with her arms folded, glaring at him. "What are you doing here?" She tried to keep her voice calm, but she heard the quiver in it.

"I'm Allison's replacement."

"You're what?" The little girls started to giggle and nudge each other. One of them raised a hand. "Yes, Heidi."

"My mommy told me that you and Mr. Shane used to be in looooove." She threw her hands over her mouth, giggling.

"Is that true?" another snickered.

Wyatt jumped up. "How come she doesn't love you anymore? Did you do something stupid, Mr. Shane?" Shane nodded his head. "Well, that's easy to fix. All you have to do is what my daddy does."

"And what's that?"

Wyatt tucked his fingers in his pockets and puffed up his chest. "He says, 'Charlene, you know when it comes to idiots, I'm the biggest one of all. But no one on this earth loves you more than this idiot.' Then he pulls her into his arms and dips her backward." Wyatt looked at the other kids. "Like they do in the movies, and gives her a big, old, sloppy kiss right on the lips." Wyatt wiped his mouth with the back of his hand and said, "Gross," before continuing his story. "Then mommy isn't mad anymore." Wyatt looked from Shane to Cassidy. "Have you tried that?"

"No, I haven't."

Wyatt folded his arms across his chest. "Why not?"

Shane winked at Cassidy. "I might have to try that."

The girls giggled more and the boys chanted, "Do it. Do it."

Cassidy let out a loud whistle. "Class is starting right now. Everyone, pick up your ropes. You boys line up behind Mr. Shane and the girls behind me."

The class had just settled down when a rope slipped around her head and dropped to her arms before tightening.

Shane pulled her to him. He winked at Wyatt, "Is this how it's done? Charlene, you know—"

"She's not Charlene," the class squealed at once. "It's Miss Cassidy."

Shane hung his head. "I'm bad."

"You got that right." Cassidy pushed away from him and stepped out of the rope, fighting between wanting to laugh or be angry.

"No wonder she's still mad at you." Wyatt shook his head. "You don't even know her name."

All the kids were shouting and trying to explain to Shane the right way to do it.

Cassidy whistled again. "Class, Mr. Shane obviously has forgotten the rules of roping. Would you like to remind him what the first rule is?"

"No roping people," they shouted.

Timmy raised his hand.

"Yes, Timmy."

"Sometimes you have to rope people."

She had a feeling she would be sorry for asking, but she did anyway. "When would that be?"

"If they're hanging off a cliff and you have to save them." Cassidy was speechless. "I saw that in a movie I was watching with my dad. Good thing the cowboy knew how to use a lasso. Otherwise, the girl would have fallen." He made a splat sound.

She could hear Shane snickering.

She smiled at Timmy. "Yes. In that case, you can lasso people. But only if it's to save their lives." Cassidy stared at Shane. It was all she could do not to lasso him and drag him out of there. She had never had a class so disrupted as this one. She glared at him. "It is never for fooling around."

She heard Shane whisper, "What fun is that?"

Ignoring him, she said, "Can we please get back to roping our dummies?" She almost died when she heard a little voice whisper, "We aren't allowed to rope the real dummy."

The sound of the door shutting behind the last parent and child vibrated through Cassidy like a warning shot. She was alone with Shane. She felt the panic brewing inside her. Without looking at him, she said, "I can put the rest of the gear away. You can go home."

"We need to talk."

She snatched the remaining lassos off the floor and dashed to the storage closet. Why did he have to ruin a perfectly good evening? "I have nothing to say to you."

"Cassidy."

She slammed the closet door and headed to the office. "Go home, Shane." She grabbed the clipboard from the hook by the door and dropped it on the desk.

"Cassidy."

She spun around. "Why are you still here?"

"Listen."

She put her hands over her ears. She knew it was childish, but she did it anyway. He took her hands grinning. "It's not about us." He crossed his heart. "It's about rodeos and bull riding."

She rolled her eyes. "What about them?"

"I want you to ride Antony this weekend."

"I'm not going."

"Why, because I'm going to be there?"

"You would be arrogant enough to think that."

"Then, why?"

"I can't leave Cleopatra for a whole weekend."

"Why not? Ben said she's improving every day and he's hopeful there will be no long-term effect."

"Ben has no right telling you anything about Cleo."

"Have you forgotten she's just as much my horse as yours?"

Cassidy glared at him. No, she hadn't forgotten they shared ownership of both horses and all their offspring. They had both signed the papers when they were in love and their future together seemed to be written in stone. "No. I haven't forgotten."

"There's no reason you can't leave her in Zeke's capable hands. If Ben wasn't around, there's no one I would rather trust the fate of my horses to than him." Shane took off his hat. "My father has said for years, he wishes he could steal Zeke away."

"Doesn't matter. I can't go."

"Why not?"

"I already withdrew."

"Why would you do that?"

"You have to ask?" She shook her head in disbelief. There was a time he would have understood without her having to say a word. Those days were long gone.

Taking a deep breath she said, "Four days ago someone tried to kill my horse. If she had died..." Cassidy's hand flew to her heart, the fear of what nearly happened threatening to choke her. Tears racked her voice. "Just the thought of what almost happened has me so tied up inside, it's hard to breathe. You of all people should understand that. I can't go this weekend, not because of Cleopatra, but because I can't bear to be that far away from her. I need to be with her. I need to be the one taking care of her. Me. Not Zeke, but me."

Shane started to reach out to her, but she stepped behind the desk and sat down. He put both hands on the desktop, leaning to look in her eyes. "I totally get it. When I think of what might have been..." he paused. "I catch myself and thank God for what is. How many times have you said what-if's are just Satan's tales to keep us off track?"

She leaned back in her chair, closed her eyes, and gave a slight nod.

"It also helps to know," he grinned, "I have someone better than Zeke and Ben taking care of my horse. I have you."

She tried not to smile when she said, "Your horse?"

He winked. "Half."

"Yeah, the back half."

"Then the back half of Antony is yours." He laughed. "Which means we are both cleaning up a whole lot of poop."

She couldn't help the small giggle that escaped. She looked at a stack of papers in the middle of the desk.

They hadn't been there earlier. She picked them up. "What's this?"

"That's what I want to talk to you about. It's time you made it to Vegas as a bull rider."

"Are you crazy? The season's half over and I'm so far down in the standings they don't even bother to waste the ink to write my name."

"Only because you don't enter enough sanctioned rodeos. And the reason for that is gone."

"How do you figure?"

"This past weekend proved that we could compete together and survive. Just being here in the same room shows we can share space and the world will go on."

"Being a little dramatic, aren't you?"

He put his fingers together. "Maybe a tad." He flashed that dimple at her and her stomach flipped. She glanced down at the papers. Looking at him was trouble. "Cassidy, I know if you competed more, you would shoot to the top in no time. Don't you think you've denied your dream long enough?"

She looked at the National Finals printout. A longing she had denied herself for years started to stir. No, this was no longer her dream. Before she could say anything, he jumped right in.

"Do you remember the year, I think you might have been three or four, not sure, but anyway, the year our dads won the World Championship? Yours for saddle bronc rider, and mine for bull riding."

She shrugged.

"I do. Guess being two years older helps me remember more." He chuckled. "Anyway, our families had a big party to celebrate and both of the buckles were displayed front and center for everyone to see. You were in awe of them. We had to keep pulling you away. I guess Ben, Jake, and I got tired of pulling you away that we stopped noticing because you somehow got my father's buckle and carried it around with you."

"Guess that caused a big to-do. Me dragging a $20,000 buckle around."

"Actually, they thought it was cute." He winked. "But then, when didn't anyone think you were cute?"

She rolled her eyes.

"Anyway, you didn't want to give it up and started to cry when they took it from you. Your dad said, 'Here, you can hold mine.' But you didn't want his. You wanted the bull rider one. One of the cowboys there jokingly said, 'I think she wants to be a bull rider.' Someone else said, 'Better kill that dream before it even starts.' But your dad picked you up and said, 'Cassidy, you can be anything you want to be. If you want to be a bull rider, don't let anyone stop you.' I know you were really young, but knowing you, I think that day the dream of having your own World Champion Bull Rider buckle was born."

"Silly dream. No woman has even made it to the National Finals."

"How many women have ever made 8 seconds? Only one other that I've heard of, other than you of course. You do it fifty percent of the time you compete. That, my *mon c*—" He stopped before he could finish the word. "That means you're Vegas worthy." He took the stack of papers from her and started leafing through.

"Here are all the upcoming rodeos. Some you're already signed up for. The others you need to send in your paperwork. The Mountain State Circuit finals are at the end of October. That gives you five months to make your move. Cassidy, you are good. No, you're better than good, you're among the elite. It's time you stop hiding your light under a bush and let the world see your dream of being the first Woman World Champion Bull Rider." He jumped up, fist-bumping the air. "I saw you ride this weekend. There's no doubt in my mind that you can do it. You're already at the top in barrel racing and are most likely to win the Women Professional Rodeo Associate All-around. Why not add the PRCA World Champion to your belt collection? What do you say?"

She stared at the paper. Could she actually do it? "If I do this and win, that means you don't."

"Cassidy, you think I don't know that?" Shane reached out and took her hands in his. "I'm the one who destroyed all your dreams." He looked into her eyes. "Please let me give this one back to you. Please." With that, he squeezed her hands, turned, and left.

She stood, watching him go. Then she sank back into her chair and leafed through the papers. He had printed them all out, every rodeo in the Mountain Circuit. She started pulling the ones for Wyoming out and laid them on the desk. That still left a whole bunch more in Colorado. She would have to ride her heart out. If she did this, it would mean no weekends off for the next five months.

She felt her heart smile. She could do it, but did she want to? She laid her head down on the desk. Did she want to do this? Her heart said "yes," then the rattlesnake slithered tighter. She could almost hear it hiss. *No. She couldn't do it. The pain of seeing him weekend after weekend would be too much.*

Chapter 16

In his rearview mirror, Shane could see the convoy of Cartwright and McDaniel trailers. A wave of happiness spread through him.

"What are you grinning about?" his co-pilot Allison asked.

"Just happy to be part of the convoy."

She looked at her brother oddly.

"I never realized how much I missed this until I came back."

"I guess." She glanced in the side mirror. "Too bad Cassidy didn't come."

"She will next week."

"Are you competing?"

"Yes."

"Then you know she won't."

"We had a little chat."

Allison almost jumped out of her seat. "You talked to her?" She put her hands over her mouth. "So it went well last night?"

He waved his hand as if to say "so-so."

"Tell me all about it."

"We didn't talk about *us*, if that's what's gotten you all giddy. We just talked about the rodeo. And I'm pretty sure she won't be avoiding them anymore."

Allison clapped her hands together. "I sure hope you're right." She glanced behind them. "Did Jake bring Antony?"

"No, I'm riding Caesar."

"Why?"

"Cleopatra still needs him."

"Cassidy said she was getting better."

"She is, but it's only been a week. Doesn't hurt to give her the extra push to get better."

"When was the last time you roped with Caesar?"

"We've been practicing."

"This ought to be interesting." She snickered. "Does Jake know his partner is on a strange horse?"

"Of course he knows." Shane flicked his sister's arm.

"Ouch." She picked up her phone. "I'm calling Mom." They both broke out laughing.

It was great to be home and great to be part of this loving family.

Cassidy had only been half surprised when Jake told her Shane would not be taking Antony with him this weekend. The Shane she had fallen in love with had always put others before himself. She shook her head. *Until he wasn't that man anymore.*

This past week she had seen flashes of the old Shane and this just proved somewhere inside he was still there.

She brushed and braided her hair. Didn't matter if he was, he would never steal her heart again. She grabbed her hat from the back of the door and hurried downstairs. The house was eerie quiet with everyone gone to the rodeo.

She poured her coffee in a travel mug, took a muffin and two apples from the counter, and headed out to the stable. She had a lot of work to do today, starting with letting Cleopatra and Antony into the paddock.

She opened both stalls and the horses followed her out. She patted Antony. "I'm counting on you to make sure she doesn't run wild." She ran her hand down Cleopatra's neck. "And you, I know you love to run, but Ben said if you take it easy for a few more weeks, you just might be able to race again." She hugged the mare. "And this year we might be going to Nationals. No more declining, no more hiding." She held out her hands, an apple in each one. While the horses ate, she couldn't help but let out a whoop. "And maybe, just maybe, I'll go not only as a barrel racer but a bull rider, too."

"Did I hear that right?" Zeke asked, coming up behind her. "Or are my old ears deceiving me?"

Cassidy laughed. "You heard it right."

Zeke pointed to the sky. "Praise the Lord, my prayers have been answered."

"You've been praying I would bull ride more?"

He laughed. "No. Are you crazy? Every time you get on a bull, I pray like a madman for God to protect you."

"Thank you. I hope you pray for the guys just as hard."

He winked at her. "Not as hard. You're my favorite."

She threw her head back and laughed. "Bet you say that to all the girls."

"Just the pretty bull riders."

"So, if not the bull riding, then what have you been praying for?"

"For you to go to Nationals." He crossed his chest. "Though if the good Lord used bull riding as the tool to get you there, who am I to question it?" He winked. "But I think it's the prodigal bull rider who's the tool."

"He did get me to at least think about it."

Zeke grinned.

She put her hand up. "Don't put anything into it that doesn't belong."

"Ask me, you belong together."

"Once upon a time." She went back into the barn and got Misty ready to ride. "I'm going to ride out toward Grampa's cabin."

He laughed. "Never could understand your fascination with that dilapidated old house."

"My great-grandfather built it."

"Well, don't be going in there. Who knows what might be living in it. Not to mention it could come tumbling down any minute."

"I'm not going all the way, just up to the ridge. I need to do some thinking."

"You always did like to figure things out on the back of a horse."

"What better place is there? With the fluid motion of the horse beneath me and God's beauty surrounding us, decisions are made easier without the chaos of life weighing you down."

Zeke patted Misty's rump. "Be safe."

When they reached the open meadow, sagebrush filled the air with that clean fresh scent of morning. Pops of color were starting to show themselves as the wildflowers peeped up from the ground and the snowy peaks of Beartooth Mountains framed the skyline.

Cassidy raised one hand in the air, keeping the other on the reins. "Thank you, God, for this beautiful morning." She rubbed Misty's neck. "You ready to let loose?" Misty's ears perked up. Cassidy threw her head back and laughed. "You know what we're about to do, don't you, girl?" With that, she nudged Misty into a full gallop. The feel of the ground flying beneath them was exhilarating.

Slowly, Cassidy let the reins slide through her hands and straightened her legs, bringing Misty out of her gallop. She rubbed between the mare's ears. "That was fun."

They left the meadow and headed up the rocky path to the ridge. At the top, she dismounted and dropped the reins on the ground, knowing Misty would not wander off. You could see for miles from here, the peaks and valleys of the land otherwise hidden between the two mountains, the stream twisting its way across the property, running into the mountain lake in front of Grampa's cabin. A mama bear was watching her cubs splashing near the edge of the water.

Cassidy hugged her arms to herself. She loved this view, loved this place. It had been here where her dreams had started. She was ten years old the first time she had ridden this far out. From this very spot, she and

Shane had discovered the old cabin in the woods. It was from here they had seen and rescued Cleopatra and Antony from the frozen lake.

After that, they had ridden out here often. It was their place. It was where they had planned their future together. They were going to restore the cabin and make it their home. Her heart constricted. That dream had died along with all of her others. Everything had been so entwined with Shane that when their relationship fell apart, she couldn't salvage any of it. She sat down on the ground and hugged her knees to her chest. Could she restore her dream of being the first Woman World Champion Bull Rider?

She laid her head on her knees. That would mean seeing him every weekend. Could her heart survive? He was right—this past weekend proved she could be around him, even if it had been torture. But in the end, life still went on.

She laid back, looking at the clouds. She needed to make a decision. "What do you think?" she called to an eagle soaring high. Misty nuzzled her arm. Cassidy sat up. "You want me to ask you, too?" she asked the horse, kissing her nose. "What do you think?" Misty nodded her head. Cassidy laughed. "I'm sort of leaning that way."

Could she do this? It wouldn't be easy, that's for sure. Bull riding never was. But then bull riding would be the easy part. Shane was the hard part. The snake around her heart tightened. *Stop it. I know who you are, you evil snake. Leave my heart alone.* She felt the constriction ease up. Could she fight the heartache?

Until last week, she hadn't seen or spoken to him since she walked up on him kissing Miranda. Cassidy groaned as the memory came flooding back. She hadn't even known she was screaming until her throat ached from the sound. She had run and by the time he finally got himself untangled from Miranda, she was already pulling out.

She'd seen him in the rearview mirror running after her. He reached the side of her truck, but then Miranda caught up to him and he stopped and just watched Cassidy drive away. She'd thought nothing could hurt as much as seeing Shane cheating... But him not coming after her? No, that had destroyed whatever was left to salvage.

Every day he remained in Vegas was another nail hammered into her heart. He had chosen the rodeo over her. By the time he returned home and wanted to talk, she'd cut him out of her life. He had proven she would never be first with him and she would not settle for second place.

He had chosen and so had she. It was over and there was nothing left to say.

Cassidy didn't realize she was crying until Misty gently nudged her face. She sat up, wiping the tears with her sleeve. "I'm okay, girl." She kissed the mare's nose. She had cried enough tears over Shane Cartwright. She was done with that, and done with letting him steal all her dreams from her.

She stood and shouted, "Look out, Vegas. I'm coming." She pulled out her phone and texted Allison.

Tell Shane I'm in.

Just because she was doing this didn't mean she had to talk to him. They were not friends. They were competitors.

Chapter 17

On Sunday evening the family was back, the horses were put away, and they had all sat down at the kitchen table. Rachel was pouring everyone coffee, while Cassidy cut the cake she'd made for them. There was a knock before the door opened and Jason Cartwright peeked in. "Hope I'm not disturbing anything."

Hank rose to greet his friend. "You must have smelled the coconut cake, clear over at your place," he said with a chuckle. "Pull up a seat."

"Sorry to drop in so late, but I have something for Cassidy."

Cassidy looked at the World Champion Bull Riding belt buckle in his hand.

He grinned at her. "Hear you're going to Nationals this year."

"I'm going to try."

"Hear you're *going*," he emphasized, "to Nationals this year."

Cassidy smiled, "Yes, sir. I am."

"That's my girl." He handed her the buckle.

"Why are you giving me this?"

"Not giving, loaning it to you, until you get your own."

Cassidy rubbed her fingers gently across the face of the buckle. "But what if something happens to it?"

Jason slapped Hank on the back. "Then I take one of his." Both men laughed.

"But—"

"Nothing is going to happen to it." He pulled out a chair and took the cup of coffee Rachel handed him. "I want you to put this in your room someplace where you'll be able to see it the first thing when you wake up, and the last thing before going to sleep, and I want you to read those words out loud." He took a sip of coffee. "Go ahead and read it."

"World Champion Bull Rider."

"Say it like you believe that's who you are."

He made her repeat it three times until she said it as if she meant it. "We have some work to do to get you ready."

"I'm ready."

"You think so?" Jason threw his head back and laughed. "Cassidy my dear, you might be in shape to ride enough bulls to keep your PRCA card year after year, but you are in no way ready for weekend after weekend of being beaten up by the beasts." He took a bite of cake. "Five A.M. tomorrow morning we get started."

Jake chuckled. "And I thought Dad was a slave driver."

Cassidy hugged the buckle to her chest. Jason winked at her. "That's the same way you held that buckle when you were three. It's about time you got your own."

"You know if I win—"

Jason held up his hand. "When you win."

"When I win, that means I've beaten your son."

Jason grinned at her. "Shane has two of them already, and nothing... well almost nothing, would make him happier than to see you win your own."

Jason finished his cake and coffee, then rose and said, "Five A.M. at the school." He was almost out the door when he turned back and added, "Wear tennis shoes and comfortable clothes, not your boots and jeans."

"No boots or jeans?"

He shook his head. "There's a new technique I want to try out, and you're the perfect guinea pig for it."

"Thanks," she said with a snicker.

Monday morning she headed into the arena at the school ten minutes early. She was surprised to see Shane and not Jason. "What are you doing here?"

"I'm all for you making history as the first Woman World Champion Bull Rider, but that doesn't mean I'm going to just sit back and watch." He winked at her. "I have a good shot at winning this year too, so if you want the title then competition starts now." He held out his hand to her. She hesitated before taking it. "May the best bull rider win." He gently squeezed.

The moment her hand touched his, a spark sped up her arm, heading straight to her heart. She quickly pulled away, wiping the hand on her leggings. Maybe this was a mistake. She couldn't train with him every day. She started to turn toward the door. No. She could, she would do this. Shane was just an annoyance she would have to deal with.

"Dad wants us inside today, said something about no need to lay in the dirt." Together they walked the short distance to the classroom. She was surprised to see that Jason had set up two rows of orange cones.

The older man looked at his watch. "Right on time. We're going to do some warmup exercises first." They started off stretching, before sprinting in and out of the cones. "Now I want you laying on the floor face down, when I yell go, jump up and run." He had a stopwatch timing them. "Now do it again." After the third time, he said, "Cassidy, that last run was two seconds faster than your first."

"How fast was the first?"

"Doesn't matter, the time. You just need to get up and run faster than the bull coming after you." She nodded. Today the bull was Shane. She had pushed herself faster trying to outrun him, but he'd still won every time.

"Shane, your best was three seconds faster." He grinned at them. "In the ring, you won't have each other pushing you. So this time get your focus off the other person and focus on getting away from the beast out to get you. One more time."

This time Cassidy imagined Shane was the bull, and when Jason shouted go, she was up and across the room before Shane had even gotten halfway. She jumped, high-fiving the air.

"For the next half hour, we're going to work on flexibility, and strengthening your knees, hips, and shoulders."

"Why aren't we riding bulls?" Shane asked.

"If I have to teach you how to ride after all these years, I haven't done my job." He rubbed his hip. "No point in risking injuries on practice. What you need more than anything is to get your mind in the game, for your muscles to be able to take a beating, and for your feet to outrun a bull." He pointed to yoga mats in front of a TV he had set up.

Shane rolled his eyes. "Yoga?"

"Focus," Jason said, pushing the remote, then went into the office.

Cassidy tried not to laugh as Shane wobbled and almost fell while attempting to stand on one leg with his arms in the air.

Grinning he said, "You think this is funny?"

"Yes."

"Obviously you've done this before."

"The church has a faith-based yoga class twice a week."

"Maybe I ought to join it."

For a second, she stared straight ahead as she switched to the other leg. "It's Monday and Thursday nights at seven." *And you better not be there.* She was glad when the DVD was over and Jason came out of the office.

"That was fun, wasn't it?" Jason asked.

"Not really." Shane half laughed. "Almost landed on my face a few times."

"Just like bull riding," Jason snickered.

The week flew by. Shane didn't show up to yoga class, but he did show up for her roping class again. When he strutted in she said, "Is this going to be a habit?"

He grinned. "Maybe."

"Please try not to disrupt the class this time."

He saluted her. "Yes, ma'am."

"Tonight we're taking them out to the pens. I think they're ready for the real thing."

Shane tossed his hat in the air. "Awesome."

The door flew open with a bang and Timmy and Wyatt came running in like a whirlwind.

"Those two remind me of Jake and me at that age."

"They sure do."

"How did our mothers handle us?"

"With a lot of love and patience."

Wyatt ran right up to Shane. "Did you kiss her yet?" He slyly nodded toward Cassidy.

"We're not starting that again. No, he didn't kiss me and he's not going to." She pointed to the other kids coming in. "Go line up."

Wyatt shuffled across the room mumbling, "They're never going to make up."

Timmy looked around. "Hey, where are the dummies?"

Wyatt looked at Cassidy and started to say something but clamped his mouth shut tight. "We'll be going outside to rope real calves tonight."

The whole class jumped up and down shouting, "Yippee!"

"Alright, calm down. I want you to get your lasso and quietly follow me." She turned and looked at Shane. "Mr. Shane will be behind you, so no roughhousing. We don't want to scare the calves."

Outside at the pens, Cassidy and Shane took turns showing the kids how to rope the calf. Wyatt raised his hand. Cassidy silently groaned when Shane called on him. "My daddy said that you two were the mixed roping champions when you were our age."

"We were."

Wyatt looked at Cassidy, folded his arms across his chest, and mumbled, "How come you quit?"

"This class is not about us," Cassidy said. "Grab your lassos, and spread out. We're going to warm up with a few practice swings before we try the calf."

Shane leaned in and whispered in her ear, "You think they talk about anything other than us at dinner?"

Cassidy bit her jaw trying to keep the smile off her face. "I would hope so," she managed to say.

A few of the children were able to touch the calf with their lasso, but none were able to rope it.

"That's a good first try. I think next week, some of you will be catching the calf." Cassidy shooed the last calf toward Shane, who was holding the gate, ready for them.

The children followed them into the barn. "We gave these four little calves a workout," Cassidy said. "Now it's time to reward them with dinner."

She started toward the stack of hay and grabbed one of the bales. Heidi put her hands on her hips and glared at Shane. "How come you're not getting the hay?"

Cassidy didn't let Shane answer. "Rule number one of owning animals," she said. "If they're yours, you take care of them, not someone else."

"You own the calves?"

"Well, no. But I work here more than Mr. Shane, so they're sort of mine."

"Anyway." Shane winked at Cassidy. "She has better muscles than I do. She does yoga." Cassidy shook her head.

Wyatt followed her wide-eyed back to the pen. "How can you carry that? Isn't it heavy?"

"I'm used to it."

"It's too heavy for my mommy and she's bigger than you."

"Your mommy grew up in town. She never had to carry hay." Cassidy handed Wyatt a flake of hay. "Here, toss this over the fence for me."

"That's what I do at home." In a few minutes, the calves were fed. "It takes a whole lot longer at home to feed the horses and cows."

"Why is that?"

"Mommy can't carry the hay, so we just carry a little bit then go back for more. It takes a long time. When Daddy did it, it was done like that." Wyatt snapped his fingers.

"No one's helping your Mom with the animals?"

"Just me."

Cassidy reached down and hugged Wyatt. "You are such a good boy. Tell your mother I'll be around tomorrow to help her feed."

Chapter 18

Cassidy groaned when she pulled up at the Blackman house and saw Shane's truck. Why was he everywhere? Wyatt Sr. was sitting on the porch in his wheelchair.

"How's it going?" she asked standing at the foot of the steps.

He pointed to the cast on his leg and arm. "Bad enough the bull came down on one leg, but he added insult to injury by going for the arm, too." They chatted for a few minutes before Wyatt nodded toward the barn. "Funny him showing up and you following on his heels, just like old times."

"No, it's not. I didn't know he was going to be here."

Wyatt grinned. "You know my son is quite mad at you."

"At me?" She placed her hand on her chest. "What did I do?"

"Not what you did, it's what you won't do."

"And what's that?"

"Let Shane kiss you."

Cassidy let out a groan. "You have to explain to him that doesn't always work."

"It does."

"Maybe for you and Charlene."

"Listen, it's none of my business, but I'm with Wyatt on this one. It can't hurt."

"You were there, you saw what he did."

Wyatt nodded. "Never in my wildest dream would I have thought you wouldn't forgive him."

"If you caught Charlene in the arms of another man, would you forgive her?"

"Not at first. But honestly, I can't imagine life without her." He glanced toward the barn. "What was that French name he used to call you?"

"*Mon coeur,*" she whispered.

"Yeah, that's it. We used to make fun of him for calling you that. He would say 'Someday, someone will be your heart and then you'll understand.' I do understand now, and I can't imagine my life without Charlene." He looked at Cassidy. "Five years is too long to go without your heart."

"He has done just fine."

"Has he?"

"I heard all about the women and the drinking. His heart never skipped a beat."

"You're wrong. When you refused to talk to him, he shut down. One night not long after it happened, we were out drinking, and being the handsome dog he is, the ladies were coming onto him. He downed his glass of beer, slammed it on the table, and said, *'The beer's not working. Maybe the women will.'* Jake tried to stop him, but Shane just said, *'I'm already in hell, might as well have fun while I'm there'.*" Wyatt crossed his heart. "It was his way to block your memory from his mind."

"Well, it worked."

"No, it didn't."

"I need to get to the barn. I promised Wyatt Jr. I would help his mom."

When she turned to leave he said, "I hope you can find a way back to your heart."

In the barn, she found Charlene and her son watching Shane. And who wouldn't want to watch him? His white Stetson was pushed up on his forehead, giving a clear shot of his rich brown eyes. The five o'clock shadow did nothing to hide the dimples in his cheeks. You could see his biceps rippling from the weight of the hay bales in each hand. He walked with a swagger as if the weight of the bales were no match for his strength.

Wyatt dashed across the barn, grabbing her by the arm and pulling her along. "Look, Miss Cassidy. Mr. Shane can carry a bale of hay in each hand, and still walk."

"I see that." Cassidy went over and took one of the bales from him.

"See, Mom?" Wyatt pointed. "I told you she could lift a bale of hay."

"What are you doing here?" Cassidy whispered to Shane.

"Helping."

"I see that, but how did you know?"

"I overhead you and Wyatt talking."

"Same old Shane, jumping right in to help out a neighbor."

"Give me a chance and you'll see a lot of me is the same."

She shook her head. "Where are we putting these?"

Wyatt ran to the corner of the barn where there was an empty stall. "In here."

Shane wiped the sweat from his forehead. "I thought it would help to have the hay closer to where they are feeding."

"Good idea." Cassidy looked around. "Do you have a wheelbarrow?"

"Yes."

"You want me to get it?" Wyatt asked, jumping up and down.

"That would be great," Cassidy said. They watched him dart off.

"That boy has way too much energy." Shane laughed.

"More now that his father isn't able to work it off of him."

Shane laughed again. "That's what my father used to do with me. Work me until I was too tired to run."

"And when was that?" Cassidy and Charlene both said at once.

"Hey, I was just a boy loving life."

She hated when he grinned, showing the deep dimples in his cheeks like he was doing now. It took her breath away. She hurried out of the barn and gulped a deep breath of air. She leaned against the side of the barn and waited for Wyatt to get back with the wheelbarrow.

The next five weeks were like a whirlwind. Jason had been right about her body. It's wasn't ready for the week after week beating it was taking. The first two weekends, she had gone in confident she would win, and she did. The third week, she drew Destroyer, and since she had ridden him before and won, she knew she would again.

But she had been wrong. She'd barely made three seconds before he tossed her like a ragdoll. When she hit the ground, Destroyer zeroed in on her. Looking in the eyes of the beast, she was forever grateful for Jason and his conditioning. She jumped up, dashing as fast as she could to the open gate.

The fourth week, she qualified but didn't win, and the fifth week found her tossed onto the hard dirt once again. Every muscle in her body screamed for a break—one she knew she couldn't take. She was moving up in the standing but not fast enough. She'd signed up for a marathon of a race and there would be no stopping until the finals. No one said this dream of hers would be easy. The hardest part had nothing to do with bulls or aches and pains—it was Shane. Avoiding him had become a full-time job.

Chapter 19

Shane poured a cup of coffee and went out to watch the sunrise. Or so he told himself. He knew Cassidy would be out feeding the horses like she did every morning of every rodeo. No one ever asked her to do it, it just somehow became her thing. But he couldn't help her, because she would just storm off, leaving him to do it himself. Which was what had happened the first week. He'd thought once she had agreed to compete alongside him it would open the door for them to talk. But no. She still refused, unless it was to talk about the rodeo, horses, or the school. Anything personal and she shut down.

He stood by the back of the trailer in the shadows watching her. He knew she knew he was there. He could tell by the way her back stiffened, but she ignored him like she always did. Six weeks and he was still no closer to breaking down her armor. She petted each of the horses before turning and going back into her trailer, never once glancing his way. He downed the coffee and went inside. He poured another cup and took it outside. This time to really watch the sunrise.

He started walking toward a small park near the parking lot. Normally it was loaded with children, but this time of day, all was quiet. He was surprised to see a man sitting at one of the picnic tables. Shane started to stroll by when the man said, "Morning."

Shane glanced at him and recognized one of the bronco riders. "Morning, Matt." He looked down and noticed the Bible on the table. "Sorry, didn't mean to disturb you."

"You didn't." Matt pointed to the bench beside him. "Care to join me?"

"Might get struck by lightning if I do."

"Nah."

"You have no idea."

"You don't strike me as the type God's going to be throwing lightning bolts at." He laughed.

"Then you haven't been paying attention the last five years." Shane pulled his hat down further on his face as if to hide from God. "I've been mighty mad at Him." Why he'd said that, he didn't know. He hadn't even realized it until the words came out of his mouth.

"Want to talk about it?"

Shane shrugged before taking the seat beside Matt.

"Let me guess. There's a woman."

"That obvious?"

"So why be mad at God?"

Shane stared at the sun peeking over the mountain-top for a long moment. Matt laid his hand on Shane's back. "It's okay if you don't want to talk about it. Just know that before you can get right with her, you need to get right with God."

Shane felt the words go straight to his core. "You're right." He nodded toward the Bible. "So, what were you reading?"

"Nothing yet. Was waiting for the sun to come up so I could see enough to read." He opened the Bible. "Let's see what God has chosen for us."

The two men read and prayed together. When they were finished, Shane stood up. "Thank you, man. I feel like a weight's been lifted." He checked his phone. "It's almost time for breakfast. Would you like to join us? My mom makes a mean plate of pancakes."

Allison jumped into the front seat of Cassidy's truck. "I'm driving home in the winner's truck."

"Glad you picked mine 'cause you like my company," Cassidy teased.

"That too." Allison grinned. They buckled up and Cassidy slowly started moving toward the highway. She looked in the side mirror—Shane's truck was three back. Her father's stock trailer and her mother's Winnebago were between them. It didn't matter that she couldn't see him, because she could still feel him. This was harder than she thought it would be.

"I can't believe you beat me again in roping," Allison said comparing their logbooks.

"And barrel racing." Cassidy gave her friend a gentle punch in the arm.

"Barrel racing is almost a given. I'm used to coming in second behind you. But in roping I've always been better. What gives?" She nodded toward the back. "You showing off for someone?"

"No way."

Allison closed the books, putting hers in her purse and Cassidy's on the seat between them. "I'm really surprised you two aren't back together."

"Why would we be?"

"Maybe because you love each other."

"I'm not having this conversation." Cassidy reached over and turned on the radio. If one more person said *"You love him,"* she was going to scream. She glanced once again into the side mirror. She could see a hint of his black truck. She did still love him... there was no denying it. She knew she always would.

But love was not enough. Trust had to be there. Respect had to be there. Putting the other person first had to be there. If you didn't have all of it, it was better to walk away before love broke your heart into a kaleidoscope of pieces never to be put back together again.

When he got bucked off that bull and it came charging at him, Cassidy had thought her heart would stop. When she made the eight seconds, she wanted to run straight into his arms like she used to do. But she had come to her senses and remembered the rodeo was his first love, not her.

Over the past six weeks, she had come to respect him again. So many times she had driven into town and seen him mowing an elderly person's yard. She had been told that each week he had been giving some of his winnings to Wyatt and Tim's family. He wasn't out chasing women or drinking. No, he was still the compassionate hard-working man she had fallen in love with so long ago. Unfortunately, she couldn't trust him.

Allison turned the volume down on the radio. "For someone who just won $30,000 you don't seem very happy."

Cassidy rubbed her right shoulder. "Just sore."

"I bet the first place you head to when you get home is the hot tub."

"You got that right. We've become best friends."

"When you were on Maddog, I overheard some men calling your ride Beauty versus the Beast."

"Maddog was a beast. That's for sure."

"I also heard them making bets on whether you would make it to the finals or not."

"I hope you told them I was."

"I did." Allison laughed.

"Then they wanted me to make a bet with them on whether you would beat my brother or not."

"You didn't."

"Of course not. I told them it wouldn't be fair to steal their money like that."

They both laughed.

Chapter 20

They had just sat down to dinner when there was a knock on the door and Shane walked in. Cassidy almost dropped the bowl of salad she was placing on the table.

"Sorry, didn't realize it was dinner time," he said.

Hank pointed to a chair. "Might as well join us."

Without hesitation, Shane took the chair beside Cassidy. She scooted her own chair away from him. Rachel raised an eyebrow at her as she placed dinnerware in front of Shane, along with a glass of iced tea.

"So what brings you out here?" Hank asked, looking at his daughter.

"I needed to talk to Cassidy about the upcoming schedule."

"Have you heard about that new invention called the telephone?" Jake teased.

"I tried, but she won't answer my calls."

"Cassidy, I thought you were past that?" Jake said. All eyes were on her.

She grabbed a piece of garlic bread from the plate in front of her and shoved it into her mouth.

"So hungry you can't even wait for us to pray?" Jake smirked at her.

She dropped the bread, glaring at him. After praying, they passed around the salad bowl, while Rachel served everyone lasagna. Cassidy stared at her plate, her appetite gone. Why did he have to sit beside her? Yes, that is where he'd always sat, but that was then, not now. There was an empty seat beside Jake. *Why didn't he sit there?* the rattler hissed inside her.

Shane gave a soft moan when he tasted the lasagna. "Mrs. M, this is delicious."

She nodded at Cassidy. "Thank her."

Shane glanced her way. "I'd forgotten what a great cook you are." He held up his fork and tipped it toward her. "Best lasagna ever."

She barely acknowledged him. She toyed with the food on her plate. "What was so important you had to rush over here to tell me?"

Hank eyed his daughter. "It can wait until after dinner."

"Fine, I'm not hungry." She pushed her chair back. "I'll be in the barn."

She grabbed her hat off the rack and pushed the door open, mumbling as she went.

"You sure do like them rude." Jake laughed.

Cassidy spun around ready to jump on her brother's words. Instead, she stormed out the door, letting it slam behind her. For a moment, she stood on the porch, one hand holding onto the post, trying to regain control. Why did she let him do this to her? Why did Shane sitting next to her twist her up in knots? She took a few deep breaths before heading to the barn. It had been eight weeks since he waltzed back into her life and it hadn't gotten any easier.

She would have thought that after all these weeks of rodeos, seeing him at the school and everywhere else she went she would be able to handle him by now. But she couldn't. Oh, she could handle him as long as he kept his distance. It was just when he was so close she could touch him that the battle inside her began.

There was no denying she still loved him. But her mind knew there was a long dark road waiting for her if she listened to her heart.

She was sitting on the rail of the fence watching Cleopatra and Antony trot around the paddock. She saw Antony's ears perk up. She pointed a finger at him. "Don't even think about it."

Shane leaned on the fence beside her. "Cleopatra is looking good."

"Ben said I should be able to take her for short rides next week."

"Awesome. Maybe Antony and I can go with you." She glared at him. "Maybe not."

"So what was so important you had to rush over here?"

"I didn't rush."

"What do you want, Shane?" She couldn't keep the irritation out of her voice.

He pulled a list from the pocket of his blue denim shirt. She glanced at it. "I've seen the list."

"I know." He pointed to the paper. "Do you realize the next one is in Boulder?"

"What?" She jumped down from the fence and grabbed the paper from him. How had she missed that? Sure enough, there in black and white was Boulder, Colorado. She knew the day would come when she would have to venture into Colorado, but she wasn't ready. What if Jennifer was there?

"Is she going to be there?"

"I don't know."

"Have you talked to her?"

"Of course not. I told you it was over between us." He started to touch Cassidy's hand but she jerked away.

"I'm not going."

"Cassidy, you have to go."

"No, I don't." She ran into the house, slamming the door behind her. Her mother looked up.

"What's wrong?"

She looked from her mother to her father. "Did you realize this weekend we would be going to Boulder?"

"Yes."

"And you didn't think to tell me?"

"I figured you knew."

"You know that's where *she* lives, don't you?"

"Yes."

"I'm not going." She bolted from the kitchen and up the stairs. She paced back and forth in her room. She had to go. But what if Jennifer was there? She couldn't hide from her forever. Cleopatra would be here, not in harm's way. Cassidy couldn't go. And back and forth she fought with herself. There was a knock on her door. "Go away."

The door opened and Shane peeked in. "Can I come in?"

She tossed a pillow at the door. "Go away."

"Cassidy, come downstairs and let's talk about this."

"I don't want to talk about it."

"Cass."

She stopped mid-step, staring at him in her doorway. "My parents let you up here?"

He grinned, opening the door wider. "I did promise to just be a minute." He glanced around the room. It was the first time he had ever gotten a peek into her domain. He was surprised to see a photo of the two of them tucked in the corner of a bulletin board filled with photographs. It looked like she had tried to hide it but he recognized it. He had the same one tucked away in his wallet, the two of them in front of Grampa's cabin. He smiled to himself... so she didn't hate him as much as she pretended to.

"I'll be down in a minute." He backed out of the room, closing the door behind him.

She took a deep breath and followed him a few minutes later. Her parents and Shane were sitting at the kitchen table drinking coffee.

Shane handed her a cup. "Figured you might need this."

She took the seat across from him. "Thanks."

"So, let's talk about this," Hank said.

"Nothing to talk about. I overreacted as always. But I am going. I will not let a bully rule my life."

Hank reached over and squeezed her hand. "That's my girl. But I promise you, you have nothing to worry about because she will not be there."

"How do you know that?"

"Do you honestly think I would put my daughter in harm's way?"

She shook her head.

"You know I have done business with her father Garrett in the past. So, I called him. Seems he was afraid of the outcome of the investigation so he shipped Jennifer off to Europe for an extended vacation."

Cassidy breathed a sigh of relief then took a sip of coffee. Her mother stood up. "How about some apple pie?"

"Thought that was for the Fourth of July picnic tomorrow," Hank said.

"I made an extra one." She winked at her husband. "Have to keep you happy."

Hank grabbed her by the waist, pulling her down on his lap. "That you do," he said kissing her.

"Really, you two. Get a room," Jake said, coming in the door.

A longing curled its way into Cassidy's heart. Would she ever have what her parents had? Without raising her head, she glanced across the table at Shane, what she thought she'd had with him. A sob crawled into her throat. She jumped up, going to the freezer. "What's pie without ice cream?"

Everyone happily chatted about the next day's big Fourth of July event. Jake, as always, wondered about who would be bringing what food.

When the last crumb of pie was gone from everyone's plate, Cassidy took the dishes to the sink. She was rinsing them and loading the dishwasher when

Shane said, "Dad, Luke, and I will be here bright and early to help set up."

Cassidy silently groaned.

He said, "Night, Cassidy."

She pretended not to hear him. Her mother answered for her. "Night, Shane."

When the door shut behind him, Rachel said, "It wouldn't have hurt to say goodnight." Cassidy kept loading the dishes. "Love is a terrible thing to waste," her mother continued.

Cassidy put the last dish in the dishwasher, shut the door, and turned it on. "I'm going to my room." She kissed her mother and father on the cheek and gave Jake a little nudge. "Goodnight, see you in the morning."

"Bright and early," Hank said.

"As always."

Cassidy frowned when she stepped into her room. He had only been there a few minutes and yet the scent of his Old Spice lingered. She couldn't believe he still wore it. She laid on the bed staring up at the ceiling. She had been twelve when she'd seen a commercial for the manly scent. So, that year for Christmas and every year after she had bought it for him. She stood by the door and took a deep whiff. She leaned her head against the door. Would it have hurt to say goodnight to him?

She crossed the room, opened the French doors of the balcony, and stepped out. The stars were shining, a wolf was howling, an owl hooted, and all seemed right with the world. But it wasn't. Not her world. A simple good night would have opened the door she had been struggling to keep shut. She couldn't give an inch without opening herself up for heartache again.

She placed her hands on the wrought iron railing, staring off into the darkness. It had been a long time since she stood there knowing Shane would be on his balcony five miles away looking toward her, and they would whisper, "Good night," knowing the other was saying it, too. And somewhere in the night their words would meet and carry them into dreams of happily ever after.

She felt a tear on her cheek. She flicked it away. There was no happy ever after. It was all just a myth. She turned to go back in, but as she went to close the door the words "Good night, Shane" slipped out. She quickly closed the door before they could carry across the night sky to him.

Chapter 21

The kitchen in the ranch house was hopping more than usual that morning. Cassidy and Allison were setting the long ranch table for breakfast. Ann was flipping pancakes on one stove while Rachel fried bacon and sausage on the other. Lydia, Zeke's wife and cook for the ranch hands, pulled cinnamon buns from the oven.

The moms were whispering and glancing back at Cassidy, then giggling. Cassidy dropped the silverware on the table, put her hands on her hips, and stared them down. "Rules of the day. There will be no miraculous pulling of my name and Shane's from the hat for games. There will be no seating us together." She stomped her foot and pointed her finger at each woman one by one. "There will be no matchmaking today. Is that understood?"

The mothers looked innocently at her. Rachel said, with a half-smirk, "We wouldn't think of it."

"Good. Because if when the names for the potato sack race are pulled and you..." she pointed at the mothers, "...pull my name and Shane's, I am going straight to the house and not coming back out until the last guest is gone. Do you hear me?"

Lydia opened the industrial sized refrigerator. She picked up a gallon of milk and turned toward Cassidy. "What about when it's only you and Shane left for the hot pepper eating contest? Are we allowed to seat you together?"

Cassidy let out an exasperated sigh. "No. We will remain in the seats we started in. As far away as possible."

Lydia put the milk back and grabbed the jam instead. Shutting the door of the refrigerator, she said, "Too many rules. Ask me, someone needs to lock the two of you in a room and not let you out until you've kissed and made up."

"Lydia!" Cassidy spun around to face the woman.

The grandmotherly matron put the jam on the table and went to the oven for the cinnamon rolls. "Just saying." She winked at the mothers. "The tack room might be a good place for that." The others laughed, but Cassidy looked appalled.

"I thought you were on my side."

"I'm on the side of true love."

"There is no such thing."

Rachel gave her daughter a sideward hug. "You know that isn't true."

"Please, can't we just enjoy the day without any matchmaking?" She looked at each one of them. "Please?"

They all nodded. She heard her mother whisper to Ann, "Just for today."

Lydia went outside and rang the bell for breakfast. Hank and Jason were the first in the door followed on the heels by Zeke. "Perfect timing, We have all the grills started. By the time breakfast is over we can put the meat on," Hank said.

Within minutes the men had taken their seats at the table, grace was said, and the day began.

By seven o'clock everyone had been fed and the preparations for the celebration were underway. Hank and Jason put beef and ham on the grills and Zeke had his famous chuckwagon beans cooking over an open fire.

The ranch hands were putting up tables and chairs. Rachel looked at the four tables they had set up for the food. "Do you think this is enough?"

"Maybe for the desserts. I think last year I ended up needing eight just for food. You know the people of this town love a good potluck."

"I hope Annette brings her potato salad. It's the best in the world," Cassidy said.

"And Mrs. Jenkins's deviled eggs," Allison added.

"I'm looking forward to Cassidy's coconut cupcakes." Ann looked at Cassidy, "You did make them, didn't you?"

She laughed. "Of course."

A little before eight, the guests who wanted to go trout fishing arrived. Rachel and Ann handed out cinnamon buns and drinks to the early arrivals. Cassidy and Allison were busy covering the food tables with paper tablecloths when Timmy and Wyatt Jr. ran up, throwing their arms around them. "Hey, what are you two doing here so early?" Cassidy asked.

"Mr. Shane is taking us fishing."

"He is?"

"Since our dads can't go he said we could be his sons for the morning."

Cassidy glanced across the lawn to where Shane was talking to some of the men. He had one foot on the step to the hay wagon, drinking a coffee. He laughed at something they said. Her heart swelled with something she refused to acknowledge. She looked down at the boys. "That is awful nice of him." She pointed to the table with the cinnamon buns and drinks. "You want one?"

They both jumped up and down. "Yes."

As they ran off, Janet laughed. "Pumping them with sugar and sending them off. Shane will be sorry he volunteered for this job."

Cassidy watched the boys run up to Shane, their excitement bubbling out of them. Shane laid a hand on each of their shoulders as if to stop their jumping. Minus the fidgeting, he seemed as excited as the boys were. His laughter drifted straight to her heart. *No.* He would not worm his way back in. She looked away. "Knowing Shane, they might be the sorry ones."

Allison added. "Hope they have dry clothes with them."

Janet looked startled. "Why?"

Cassidy and Allison started to giggle. "Shane thinks it's fun to try and catch the trout barehanded."

"Oh my, I better call Charlene and tell her to bring Wyatt a change of clothes." Janet hurried off.

She watched Shane drive the tractor pulling the wagon full of fishermen and women until it disappeared over the hill. Relief filled Cassidy. Now she could relax for a few hours without worrying about bumping into him.

"If I were a single woman and that man had eyes for me, I would do everything I could to grab him before someone else does," Lydia said as she scooted behind Cassidy.

Cassidy looked at the woman.

"Just saying that's what I would do."

Cassidy shook her head.

By midafternoon, the party was hopping. There was enough food to feed the whole town, which was a good thing since most of them came. Games of volleyball and horseshoes were in full swing.

Cassidy was leading the children one by one around on horseback when Luke came up beside her. "You missed the potato sack race."

"I've been busy."

"I see that." He looked at the long line of children still wanting to ride. "Have you eaten anything yet?"

"Not before the hot pepper contest."

"Don't know why you torture yourself by eating those."

She laughed. "I like being the winner."

"This year you have some real competition."

"Only if he's kept up with eating them."

"You're both crazy."

"I've been told that." She giggled as she took a little girl off the horse, and lifted a young boy into the saddle.

She made sure he was seated before leading the horse around the corral.

Luke glanced at his phone. "I'll take over here so you can go get ready for the contest."

"You don't want to watch?"

"No way." He chuckled. "Makes my stomach hurt just thinking about it."

Cassidy laughed. "Just think what it does when you eat them."

"I'll leave that to the fools."

Cassidy tossed her head back laughing.

The contest started with twenty men and women brave enough to compete. Each round of peppers was hotter than the last. Everyone had a glass of milk in front of them. Once you needed the milk to cool the burn, you were out.

It was now down to four people—Zeke, Shane, Hank, and Cassidy. Lydia handed each of them a ghost pepper. The men took a tiny nibble, Zeke and Hank immediately grabbed their glasses of milk and downed them. Cassidy took a deep breath then popped the whole thing in her mouth, eating it as quickly as she could. Her mouth was on fire, and she could barely breathe from the heat. She glanced down the table at Shane. His face was red, beads of sweat dotted his forehead, but he didn't reach for the milk. So neither would she.

The crowd clapped as they both signaled for the next pepper. Lydia gave them a few minutes before handing each of them the viper. Cassidy looked at Shane. He held the pepper up as if toasting her and popped it in his mouth. Cassidy quickly did the same. As she bit into it, her mouth exploded with fire. It was so hot she wouldn't be surprised if smoke came out of her mouth. Yet neither of them touched the milk. She had no doubt her face was as red as his.

She inhaled and exhaled, trying to cool the burn. Suddenly Shane was sitting next to her. Lydia raised her hands as if to say, *"It wasn't me."* Cassidy closed her eyes. What wasn't already in turmoil from the peppers had jumped on board this sinking ship. Her heart raced, her stomach churned, her head spiraled out of control. She jumped from her seat, reached for her milk, and drank it then backed away from the table.

Lydia raised Shane's hand. "We have a new pepper champion." Shane quickly downed his milk. He turned to her. "Thanks. Don't know if I could have handled the scorpion."

Her father handed her another glass of milk. This time she let the milk sit in her mouth for a moment to cool the burning taste buds before swallowing.

Just before nightfall, everyone loaded into the three hay wagons and headed to the north ridge to see the Cody fireworks display. Cassidy made sure she was not on the wagon Shane was driving. When they got to the ridge, her brothers had a bonfire going not only for s'mores but also to keep the wild animals away. She watched to see where Shane would settle down before grabbing Allison by the hand and going to the opposite end of the crowd. Luke, Willow, and a few of their friends followed along.

As the fireworks lit up the night sky, he couldn't help but search for her. He found her seated between Allison and Luke... Luke, always Luke. Shane felt a slow burn spread across his chest. What was going on with them? He shook his head. They were friends, that's all. Wasn't it? He glanced at the others on the blanket. They were all laughing and having a good time. He ached to join them, but knew she would go somewhere else if he did.

The blast of light filled the sky and the crowd clapped. He watched Cassidy lay her head on her knees. Firework after firework, she never lifted her head. What was that about? He wondered if she remembered what he'd said to her years ago. He'd been sixteen, and they sat right here on this very ridge cuddled together, so much in love. He'd whispered in her ear when the first firework went off that the explosion of color was how his heart felt every time he saw her. That night he gave her his class ring and promised her his heart forever and always. He wanted to rush over to her now, tell her he'd meant every word.

Shane got up and slipped away from the crowd. He didn't need light to know where he was going. He knew by heart where their tree was. His finger found their initials and he traced the heart around it. He leaned his head against the tree. *Please God, I can't do this without Your help. I know with all my heart that You chose Cassidy for me, but I messed it up big time. Help me show her I do love her and I will cherish her forever and always. Please show her the way to forgive me.*

Chapter 22

Cassidy was tossing hay to the calves at the school when Shane slipped up behind her and grabbed her by the waist. Electricity sparked through her body. Cassidy spun out of his hands, giving him a dirty look. "Don't touch me."

He held his hands in the air. "Forgot myself for a minute."

"Don't do it again. What are you doing here?" She turned back to the calves. "Thought you were out rounding up cattle with the others."

"I was until I checked my phone." He pulled it from his pocket. "Have you checked the standings?"

"No."

He held the phone out for her, pointing to her name on the list. "In less than three months you've moved up to the top thirty."

"And that has you shirking your duties because...?"

He laughed. "Hey, my dad agreed I needed to show you."

Cassidy shook her head. "I still have a long way to go."

"Yeah, but don't you see this just proves you can do it?"

"Yes, I'm moving up in the Mountain Circuit but I think I started too late to make the top fifteen money-winners in the PRCA. I hate to disappoint you, but I don't know how I can earn enough money to make it to the NFR."

"You just can't fall off any more bulls." He started to reach out and touch her but pulled his hand back.

"That was always the plan." She rubbed her hip. "Falling off is no fun."

"Don't I know it," he chortled. "Why do you think half the cowboys around here limp?"

"For sympathy."

He threw his head back laughing. The sound of his rich laughter warmed its way straight to her heart. She couldn't look at him because she knew those dimples would be her undoing. Why did he still affect her like this? They had no future. She couldn't trust him. She glanced toward the sky. *Why can't You take this away? Give me a love that is real, not fake.* She flung hay over the fence. She brushed it off her hands and clothes and turned to go into the school.

"Look." He pulled a paper from his back pocket. "There are two weekends where we have a one-day rodeo. I'm thinking those weekends we double up."

"What?"

"Hear me out." He tipped his hat further back on his head. "We're already signed up for Lamar, Colorado, and that same weekend there's a Friday night rodeo in Sterling. We could do both. And—" He smiled sheepishly at her. "We could add a few in Montana. It wouldn't count toward the Mountain Circuit standings, but it would toward the NFR." He handed her another list.

"Are you crazy?"

He grinned. "Yes." He nudged her with his elbow. "We're rodeo brats. What's a three-hour drive between events to us?"

"It's not the drive I'm thinking about."

"Listen, on the extra rodeos, you don't worry about barrel racing unless you want to."

"I'll think about it."

He handed her another sheet of paper. "Think quick. We need to get our applications in soon."

She rolled her eyes and shook her head. "Fine."

"Yes!" He jumped in the air.

"You are awfully excited for someone who is going to get beat."

He held his hand out to her. "May the best bull rider win."

She slipped her hand into his, then quickly pulled it away. Touching him even briefly had to be off-limits.

The whirlwind of a season was coming to a close. Cassidy loaded Cleopatra into the trailer along with Antony and Misty. "Can you believe this? We're heading to the Mountain States Circuit Finals." Cleopatra pranced into the trailer. "You're excited too, huh? I guess you are because this is only your second race since May. We are going to do just what we did last time. Most of the weekend you are going to be relaxing, while Antony does the heavy running. I'm saving you for the last race. I know Ben said you were as good as new, but I don't want to take any chances. I need you perfect for Vegas." She stroked her mare's neck. "The plan is to win both bull rider and barrel racing and qualify for Vegas."

She made sure Cleopatra was secure in the trailer. Then she turned and hugged Antony. "I know you've gotten me here this year, but you know Cleo and I are a team." Antony neighed and nodded his head. "I knew you would understand."

In the first race on Friday night, Antony soared around the cloverleaf as if he had wings on his feet. Their time of 14 seconds won them the round.

She put on her chaps and vest and headed toward the chutes. She took a deep breath. She needed to win not just this ride, but all three rounds to guarantee a spot in Vegas. If there was such a thing. She stopped walking. Not for the first time, she wondered if she won, would that knock Shane out?

"Can't worry about that," Shane said coming up behind her.

"About what?"

"Whatever it is you're thinking."

"How do you know I'm thinking anything?"

"Why else would you just stop dead in your tracks?" He grinned. "If you're worried about beating me, don't be."

"I'm not." She put her hands on her hips. "If you must know, I was thinking about how good it will feel to beat you."

He laughed. "May the best bull and rider win." He winked at her. "Vegas, here we come."

"Let's hope."

"Cassidy." He pointed his finger at her then back at himself. "The two of us are the ones with targets on our backs. We are the ones to beat." He slipped his arm around her shoulder. "Let's go show them why that is."

For a second she allowed the warmth of his arm to fill her with strength, before slipping away from him. "You're on."

They rode in the order of their standings, which meant she and Shane would be the last two riders of the night. She sat in a corner twirling the spokes of one of her spurs, watching and waiting,

"Cassidy." She didn't even look up at Miranda. "Do you have a few minutes to do a pre-ride interview?"

She sighed. "Yes, of course." Cassidy plastered a smile on her face. One day, she would have to forgive the woman, but not today.

Miranda looked around. "I was hoping to find you before *Sports Illustrated* did."

"What?"

"They're here looking to interview you."

"Why? I haven't won yet."

"No, but everyone is rooting for you."

"I'm sure not everyone." Cassidy stood up, smiling. "But that is a nice thought."

Miranda nodded to her cameraman. "I'm here with Cassidy McDaniel, the first woman to ever make it to a finals event as a bull rider." She turned to Cassidy, pointing the mic at her. "How does it feel to have come this far?"

"Honestly, it's been such a whirlwind I haven't had time to stop and think about it. If anything, it's been surreal."

The interview lasted a few more minutes before Jake waved to tell her it was time to get ready. "I need to go."

Miranda turned off the mic. "Good luck, Cassidy. I hope you win."

"Thanks." She grabbed her gear and hurried over to Jake. They walked to the chutes where her father, Jason, and Shane were standing.

"Only two riders left, Tanner and Jerry, before the real showdown begins." He pointed to the left chute where she would be. He fist-bumped her. "We got this."

Jason gave her a big hug. "I know I should be rooting for my son, but..." He winked at Shane. "...I'm rooting for the pretty one this time."

Shane started toward the right chute. Even with his back to her, she heard him say, "Me too."

Her father pulled her into a bear hug. "I'm so proud of you."

"Thanks, Dad."

Shane looked over his shoulder. "Hey, you two go back to your bulls and horses and let her focus. She's got this."

They nodded and walked away. The gate flew open and Jerry and his bull shot out. Now it was her turn. She watched as they moved Fireball into place. Once they had him settled, she climbed the gate. "It's you and me again."

"I hate this bull," Jake said.

She leaned over and patted the bull's head. "I don't. He gets me lots of points."

"When you stay on."

"Tonight is that night." She climbed over and went through her routine before leaning over and talking to the bull. "Tonight you can kick and do your best to get me off, but I'm not falling. Do you hear me? Eight seconds is all I ask."

She sat up and positioned herself. Cassidy nodded and the gate flew open. They were out of the chute like the devil was after them. The bull kicked high to the left before all four feet left the ground. She felt the *thug* of the bull's weight jar through her as his feet slammed back to earth. The impact shifted her off-center. She hung on tight, righting herself and moving with the motion of the bull.

When the buzzer sounded the eight seconds was over, Cassidy jumped from the bull's back and landed on her feet as bullfighters wrangled the bull out of the ring. She removed her helmet and her long black hair fell across her shoulders and down her back. As she hurried out of the ring, her score of 91.5 was broadcast. "Yes," she silently shouted to herself. That was the best score of the night so far. Now it was time to watch the last rider, Shane.

Shane was on Loco, who was as crazy as his name. All of the bulls this weekend were top bulls. There would be no easy rides for anyone. So far, there had only been five qualified rides, including hers.

She held her breath as the gate opened and Shane and his bull hit the ring kicking. Shane's hat hit the ground seconds later, but he held his seat until the buzzer sounded. He jumped from Loco's back grinning. He ran and grabbed his hat and waved it at her. When his score of 91 was announced, the audience was in shock. A woman had won round one. She had beaten him by half a point.

This was the last ride of the weekend, and she had drawn Loco, the same bull Shane had the first day. This was the longest eight seconds of the whole season. Make this, and a trip to Vegas was almost guaranteed.

Cassidy nodded and the gate flew open. She hung on as Loco kicked with his hind legs then made a sudden drop with his front legs, trying to get her to jerk her head back. This bull was smart. He knew that where her head went, her body would follow. But she was not falling for that, or for anything he threw at her today. Cassidy kept her eyes right in front of her hand, her legs squeezed tight against the bull's body, her left hand raised high.

The buzzer sounded and Cassidy let go, falling to the ground. The bullfighters were there seconds before Loco's feet could come down on her, chasing him out of the ring.

Cassidy pulled her helmet off and her eyes drifted to the scoreboard. She was the last rider of the Finals. She needed a 92 or better to knock Shane out of first place.

"Ninety-three," the announcer called out and the audience went still. Then they erupted into cheers. She had done it. Cassidy threw her helmet in the air. A woman had just won the Mountain Circuit Bull Riding event. Tears flowed down her face. She had done it.

Shane ran up, lifting her from the ground and twirling her around. "You did it!"

She put her hands on his shoulders. It was all she could do to not reach down and kiss him. "Put me d-down." Her voice betrayed the want inside of her.

Once her feet hit the ground, she gave him a quick hug. The scent of Old Spice mingled with bull and sweat, filling her senses with longing. She pushed away. "We did it. Thank you. Without you, I wouldn't be here."

He grinned. "Vegas, here we come."

"Does this mean we get to relax a little?"

Cassidy's father came up behind her, squeezing her shoulders. "Very little." He laughed.

Two days of competing and the Mountain Circuit Finals were over. All that was left was the awards ceremony. She had beat the odds and won. No one had been surprised when she won barrel racing, but she had shocked not only the circuit but the world by winning bull riding. She hugged the buckle to her chest. The thrill of victory was bittersweet. She had beaten Shane.

Chapter 23

Cassidy paced the long hallway away from the bullpens. Her gut was tied up in knots. She felt like she was going to throw up. She leaned her hand against the wall. *Pull yourself together. It's just another ride.* She half-heartedly laughed at herself. *Just another ride?* This was for the World Championship. If she pulled this off, she would be the first woman to do it.

Her hand flew to her stomach. She made it this far. No matter what happened she had already made history. She, Cassidy McDaniel, had proven that women were just as capable bull riders as men. Hadn't the last eight months shown that? *So why are you such a wreck?*

She felt his hand on her back. Without looking up, she said, "What?"

"What's going on?" Shane asked. She shrugged her shoulders. Shane turned her to face him. "Cassidy, this is just another ride."

"Ha."

He grinned. "Okay, so maybe it's a little different than the rest."

"You think?"

"I don't understand. You never let nerves get to you."

"You don't understand what's riding on this."

"Tell me."

"Everyone is watching... not just the people here. Millions of people are watching on TV. Half of them praying I fail so they can say 'See, I told you a woman doesn't belong in this sport.' And the other half is wanting to make me a hero." She shook her head. "I'm no hero."

"Like it or not, you already are a hero to millions of little girls and women out there who were afraid to follow their dreams. You showed them they can."

"I don't—"

He placed his hands on either side of Cassidy, pinning her to the wall without even touching her. Old Spice wrapped around her, filling her with longing. She closed her eyes, fighting the emotions swirling through her.

"Too late," he was saying. "It doesn't matter what happens today. The last eight months have carried you to the top of the hero mountain." He cupped her face in his hands. "You went from not even being worth the ink, as you said, to even be counted in the standings, to being in the top three going into this final event. No, Cassidy, your hero status is already established. Today is just the icing on the cake."

She lowered her eyes to a patch on his vest. "What if I win?"

"This whole place will erupt, unlike anything you have ever seen."

"Then you lose."

Shane pulled her into his arms. "*Mon coeur*, I will be leading the celebration." He lowered his mouth to hers. The feather touch of his lips on hers sparked a trail of passion through her. She could feel her heart melt into his—this was her dream. She put her arms around his neck, pulling him closer. For a moment nothing else mattered. This was where she belonged.

Then reality struck as the rattler coiled around her heart, squeezing the air from her. She pushed him away, wiping her hand across her mouth. "What are you doing?"

"What I should have done five years ago," he said.

She stomped her foot. "Five years ago, you were enjoying kissing someone else."

"You're wrong. That kiss was never enjoyable."

Humph. She grabbed her gear and stormed off. How dare he kiss her? *How dare you enjoy it*, she screamed to herself. She was not a toy for him to play with. No, that two-timing Romeo was not winning today.

Shane leaned against the wall watching her go. He wasn't sorry he had kissed her. No way would he ever regret kissing Cassidy. He touched his lips. For a second, she had returned that kiss. He glanced upward. *Thank You for the flicker of love I felt from her. Now to get it moving a little faster would be much appreciated.*

Jake hurried up to him. "Don't know what you did to make her so mad, but man you are going down."

"I kissed her."

"You what?" Jake tossed his hat in the air. "Well, it's about time."

"Was it? You see how she felt about it."

"Mad enough to win."

Shane grinned. "Yeah."

Cassidy was furious as she put on her chaps and spurs.

"Don't forget to let your hair down," Shane said, flicking her braid as he walked up with Jake.

"Don't touch me."

He put his hands up. "Just don't want there being any doubt you're a woman when you win."

Jake touched her helmet with his foot. "Like that vine of roses on her helmet isn't proof enough."

"Will you two go away?"

"What?" Jake put his hand over his heart. "I thought I was your flankman."

She glared at him. "You are, but I need to focus and don't need you two bothering me. Come back when it's time for me to get in the chute."

Cassidy watched them amble away. She had fifteen minutes before she had to get in the chute. Fifteen minutes to scream at her heart for betraying her. No, she had to focus on this ride. Shane Cartwright was a distraction she couldn't afford right now. She needed to have the best ride of her life if she was going to win. And winning was what she planned on doing. The rattler shook its tail. *Plans. We like plans.* "Shut up," she yelled. *Get out of my head, get out of my heart, go away.*

It was time. Jake gave her a hand up as she climbed over the chute. She had drawn Destroyer.

"I hate this bull," Jake said.

"Other than you hate them all. I don't get it. He's an awesome bull."

"Ask the bull riders who have hit the ground how great he is."

"Don't have to ask. I was one of them."

"I remember."

She leaned over and patted the bull's back. "Yup, it's me again. Right now it's two to one, your favor, but today we even the score."

She slipped slowly down on Destroyer's back. Jake helped her tighten the bull rope around the bull and held it taut while she rubbed it, getting the rosin warm. The crowd was cheering as Justin made 8 seconds. Cassidy had to focus on her ride, tune everything out around her. No noise, no crowd, just woman against beast. She could do this. No, she *would* do this.

She mentally recited the words she had been saying every morning, *"I am the World Champion Bull Rider,"* over and over in her head. She leaned forward and whispered to the bull, "I know you remember me. I remember you, too. The last time you tossed me like a sack of potatoes in less than two seconds then chased me halfway across the ring. Not today. I know you love it when the adrenaline rushes through your veins. Well, I'm the cause of it. So we are going to join your adrenaline and mine together." She patted the side of the rock hard animal. "Today you and I are going to make history."

Cassidy readjusted, made sure her hand was tight in the rope, focused her eyes on the back of Destroyer's neck, and took a deep breath, trying to still the pounding of her heart. It was just her and a bull, no crowd, no world champion. Just a girl and her beast. This was it. Her dream coming to life. The impossible was possible. A whoop welled up inside of her. She let it loose, then nodded her head.

Like a rocket, Destroyer flew from the chute, his hind legs kicking almost straight up. He dropped his front legs so fast the vertical force almost pitched Cassidy off. But she hung on.

The bull twisted to the right. All four feet left the ground. When they touched down, Cassidy felt the jar, but she refused to fall. She kept her left hand held high, her legs tight against the body of the beast, and allowed her body to react to his movement.

When Destroyer lurched forward, she moved with him. When he twisted to the right, she hung on. He did a half-turn then quickly spun to his left... she barely heard the buzzer over the roar of the crowd.

She had done it. Cassidy released her grip on the rope and jumped off, landing on her hands and knees. The bullfighters rushed in between her and Destroyer. She looked the beast in the eyes and smiled before rushing to safety.

In the middle of the ring, Cassidy pulled her helmet off, tossed it in the air and jumped as high as Destroyer had moments ago. She did it. She glanced up at the scoreboard... 94, her best ride ever.

She ran from the ring straight into Jake's arms. "You did it!" Laughing, he lifted her, spinning her around. "A 94, unbelievable."

Her parents and Ben came rushing up. "That's my girl. I knew you could do it," her father said. "And on the bull of the year, no less." Hank hugged his daughter. "Don't know how anyone is going to top that."

"I haven't won yet. Tanner and Shane still need to ride."

"Doesn't matter. You made history by being the first woman to ever make 8 seconds at the National Rodeo," her mother said.

Cassidy was led over to the winner's box. In all the excitement, she had missed Tanner, but his score was barely 90. There was one rider left and that was Shane. She placed her hand over her heart. *Please keep him safe and give him a good ride.* She wanted to win, but in her heart, she knew she wouldn't be disappointed if he did. It was out of her hands now. She had given it her best shot, and that was all that mattered. The win was just a bonus.

Shane had drawn Moonwalker, the bull in second place for the bull of the year. Very few had successfully ridden him, and if Shane could do it, he very likely could outscore her. It all depended on his ride. The chute opened and they shot out. Shane's hat flew off seconds after he entered the ring. Moonwalker was doing all he could to get Shane off his back. He was spinning and kicking like a rabid beast.

When the buzzer sounded, Cassidy jumped to her feet clapping and cheering like the rest of the crowd.

He hit the ground running. His eyes drifted to hers, a grin on his face. He mouthed, "We did it!"

Her heart shouted back, *"We did!"*

There was dead silence as the crowd waited for his score. They all knew whoever won this last event won it all.

When his score of 93.5 flashed, the crowd went wild. Someone grabbed Cassidy and before she knew what was happening she was lifted on Tanner and Justin's shoulders and paraded back into the ring. She had made history. Cassidy McDaniel was the first Woman World Champion Bull Rider.

Shane ran up to them jumping and high-fiving her. "You did it!"

"We did it," she said as the guys put her down. She gave Shane a quick hug. "Thank you for giving me back my dream."

He whispered, "There are other dreams I want to restore, too."

She pushed away from him, shaking her head. "This is enough." She allowed herself to be swept away from him. But the thrill of the win was dimmed by the ache in her heart. If only she could trust him.

Chapter 24

Cassidy was driving through town when she saw Shane putting up Christmas lights on the Jenkins house. Her heart gave a little leap. *Stop that,* she rebuked it, but she couldn't keep the smile from her face, or her fingers from touching her lips.

It had been a week since National Finals, and with all the baking, decorating, and shopping for Christmas, Cassidy had not seen him. Not even when she had gone over to the Cartwrights' to return Jason's buckle. And since there were no classes at the school until after the New Year, there was no chance of running into him there. It surprised her how much she missed seeing him.

This morning when she woke up and realized it was Friday and there was no rodeo—which meant no Shane— her heart had nearly stopped beating. She scolded herself. *Pull your head out of wonderland and get a grip.*

Fifteen minutes later, she stood waiting in the hospital lobby for the elevator. Christmas carols played softly in the background. The door opened and Mr. Triplett stepped out. "How are you?" she said hugging the sweet man. "Merry Christmas."

"Merry Christmas to you, too. You heading up to see Mr. Jenkins?"

"Yes, how is he?"

"Doing good. Itching to get out of here. He said he had to put up Christmas lights."

"Well, I'll let him know I saw Shane doing just that on my way past his house."

"That boy has always had the gift of service." Mr. Triplett smiled. "It's good to see the two of you back together."

Cassidy frowned. "We are not back together."

Mr. Triplett took a step back in surprise. "I assumed since you were together at church, you had forgiven him."

She shook her head. "We'll never be together again."

"Why?"

"I can't trust him."

Mr. Triplett looked at her for a long minute. "That is truly a shame. I remember back when I was your Sunday School teacher, and we were studying first Corinthians chapter thirteen, you looked across and said, 'I will always love Shane like that'."

"I was fifteen years old."

"You also added, 'Nothing will ever break us apart'."

"I was naïve."

"Cassidy, do you remember the verses?"

She nodded.

"You need to forgive him."

"I have forgiven him. The issue is I can't trust him."

Mr. Triplett took her hand in his. "There is no can't in love."

"But—"

"No, Cassidy. It's not that you can't. It's that you won't. Love does not '*keep a record of wrong doing.*' '*It always protects, always trusts, always hopes, always perseveres. Love never fails.*' I don't know one person who knew the two of you that didn't believe for one second that the love you shared was a gift from God. If what we believe is indeed true, I have a question for you. When God gives you a gift, don't you think you should take it?"

Cassidy nodded. She could feel tears glistening in her eyes.

"So, why won't you love him?"

She stared at the floor for a long moment, his words swirling around her heart. *"It's not that you can't. You won't."* She knew he spoke the truth. She had refused to trust Shane, refused to ever be his friend. Refused to listen to her heart. Refused to listen to God. Her heart clenched with pain.

Mr. Triplett lifted her face with his finger. "Cassidy, pray about it."

Cassidy put her arms around his waist. "I will."

Cassidy left the hospital, her mind and her heart battling with each other to be right. That ugly rattler squeezed her heart until she thought she couldn't breathe. She parked then went right to the barn and saddled Cleopatra.

"Where are you going?" her father asked, coming up behind her.

"Cleopatra and I need a ride."

"Looks like a storm is coming so don't be long."

Cassidy looked up at the dark clouds moving in from the north. "Still a good ways off. We'll be back before it hits."

Cassidy mounted her mare and headed out toward Grampa's cabin. She stroked Cleopatra's neck. "I need to do some thinking, girl, and you need to stretch those legs. I promise if I feel you growing tired we will turn around and come right back."

Cleopatra pranced as if to say, *I'm good for the ride.*

"We are not going to run, if that's what you're thinking. This is just a slow easy ride."

Mr. Triplett's words kept repeating themselves over and over again. There was no doubt that she loved Shane. She had for as long as she could remember. And who wouldn't love him? He was kind, funny, compassionate to people and animals, patient, had integrity, worked hard. He was handsome, and stirred a passion in her no one else could ever do. No, loving him had never been the problem.

He had betrayed her. Broken her heart. How could she ever trust him again? A soft voice in her head said, *"But you do trust him."*

She glanced skyward. *Do I?*

She fought with herself all across the meadow. Cleopatra made the turn toward the ridge. Cassidy turned her away. "Don't think you're ready for that steep grade yet. We'll just ride down into the valley and around. I know it's longer, but it's an easier ride." She twisted Cleopatra's mane in her fingers. "Once we get to the lake we'll rest a bit before heading back." The mare took a stutter step. Cassidy stroked the horse's neck. "I know the lake holds bad memories for you, but trust me, I won't let it or anything harm you." Cassidy pulled the sheep wool collar of her coat up around her neck as a cold breeze stirred up.

Once they passed the shelter of the mountain and started down into the valley, there would be no protection from the wind. For a moment, she thought about turning back, but the lake was only ten minutes away. The clouds were still hovering over Montana, so they had plenty of time. And if by chance it got too bad, they could wait it out in Grampa's cabin. She smiled. It wouldn't be the first time they had holed up there. "Remember that time we were out here with Shane and Antony, and the sky let loose a torrential rain?" Cassidy couldn't keep the giggle from bubbling out. "The four of us crowded into the tiny cabin until it was over. After that, Shane always made sure there were logs for a fire inside." There were so many memories wrapped inside that cabin. Were there more to be made? She hoped so.

Cassidy had been wrong; life without Shane was not really living. They belonged together. Her heart filled with a warm glow as she unlocked her love for him from its prison, and allowed the wind to carry the angry away.

That same wind started howling. Or was that a bobcat? She pulled the reins, slowing Cleopatra to a trot. The trees on the steep hill to the ridge were bare of leaves, making it easy to see there wasn't anything hiding there. The last snowfall showed no sign of fresh tracks. Cassidy looked to her right. It was impossible to see if any animals were lurking in the dead barnyard grass. It waved in the wind, but it didn't look like anything was moving it from below.

She patted Cleopatra. "This storm must be a bad one. Even the animals are in hiding." She looked at the clouds. Now they were moving fast. "We need to hurry and get you some water, then head back before those clouds drop their fury on us." She squeezed her legs into the mare's sides.

Cleopatra neighed and stretched her own legs into a gallop. The icy air blew in Cassidy's face, stinging her eyes as they rounded the base of the mountain into the open meadow. She reached to pull her hat lower on her forehead—too late! She didn't see the small herd of elk until the largest one let out a loud bugle. Cleopatra reared up, taking Cassidy by surprise. The reins slipped from her hands and she fell, hitting her head on a rock.

Shane was in the barn getting ready to feed the animals before the storm hit when his world dropped out from under him. He couldn't breathe. He fell to one knee. *Cassidy.* He grabbed his phone and dialed her number. It rang several times before going to voice mail.

He quickly called her mother. "Mrs. M, where's Cassidy?" He tried to keep the tremble out of his voice.

"She went for a ride." She paused. "Why?"

"Something's wrong." He jumped up. "I'll be there shortly. Have Jake saddle Antony for me." He tried not to panic, but he knew something bad had happened. *Please God, lead me to her. Keep her safe until help arrives. You gave us this gift for just this reason, thank You.*

Shane jumped out of his truck at the McDaniels' and ran into the barn. Jake had already saddled Antony, and he and Hank were saddling their horses.

"No. You stay here," Shane said jumping on Antony. "Let me find her first." He put his hand on his chest. "It's bad. You might need to bring the truck."

"How will you find her without help?"

Shane pointed to the sky. "I have help." With that, he spun Antony around and out of the barn. He squeezed Antony with his calves and heels. "Our girls are in trouble." They didn't even wait for Hank to open the gate. They jumped the fence and flew across the field.

He knew where to find her—Grampa's cabin. Before they had gone a mile the snow started coming down fast and hard. *Please let her have made it into the cabin and not be laying in the snow somewhere.*

Shane made the turn to head up across the ridge when Antony balked. "Come on, boy. This is the shortest way."

Antony came to a dead stop. "You know they wouldn't have gone that way?" Shane nudged him. Antony neighed and shook his head. Shane looked toward the ridge, then toward the valley. *Which way, God?* Shane felt peace come over him as he loosened up the reins. "Okay, boy, go find them."

Antony took off. It wasn't long before they could hear Cleopatra's loud neighing. Antony's long legs flew across the field but it seemed like they were crawling. Time stood still until they rounded the bend and Shane saw Cassidy lying still on the ground, her horse standing guard over her.

"NO! NO! NO!" Shane jumped out of the saddle screaming before Antony even came to a stop. Blood was pooled by her head. She wasn't moving. His heart stopped beating. He couldn't breathe. Dropping to the ground beside her, he prayed, *Please don't take her from me.*

He placed his cheek near her mouth and nose. Air. He felt air. *Thank you, God.* Tears clouded his eyes. "Cassidy," there was no response. "Hang in there, *mon coeur.* I'm here. I'm here." He brushed the hair from her face. "I don't know if you can hear me, but I want you to know, if I could, I would pick you up and hug you so tight I'd never let you go. But I don't know how bad you are hurt, so I can't do that." Her hat lay not too far away. He picked it up and angled it across her face to keep the snow off. "Okay, here goes." He took a deep breath. "I'm going to check you over. I'll be as gentle as I can, and I'll try not to move you."

Quickly he assessed the situation. Her arm was at an odd angle beneath her. He felt her legs, her neck, and as much of her back as he could without moving her. When he touched her right arm, she moaned. The sweet sound of life filled him with hope. He kissed her gently. "I'm going to get you a blanket then call for help." It was only when he started to rise that he realized Antony and Cleopatra were standing right beside them, acting like a windbreaker. He barely had to move to get the bedroll off Antony's back.

Shane tucked the heavy blanket around Cassidy as best as he could. Then he grabbed his phone and called Hank. "I found her. We're near Grampa's cabin, on the lower side by the lake. She's unconscious and I'm pretty sure her arm is broken."

"Can you get her into the cabin?"

"No. With her being unconscious, I'm afraid to move her."

"Ben is with me. He said keep her as warm as you can."

"Hurry!" Shane hung up and looked around. Cassidy moaned again. He pulled the blanket up around her neck. "I'm here, *mon coeur*. I'm here."

Her eyes flickered open. "Shane," she barely whispered, then tried to say, "Cleo—" and her eyes rolled back then shut.

"Cassidy, can you hear me?"

A weak "yes" escaped her lips.

"Cleopatra's fine. I need to get you out of the snow. Can you tell me what hurts?"

"Arm," she struggled to say. "Head."

"Nothing else?"

"No."

"Then I'm going to get you into Grampa's cabin. When I lift you, if you feel pain anywhere you need to tell me."

"Okay."

He took the scarf from around the band of her hat. "This is going to hurt." He slid the scarf under her back and as gently as he could wrapped it around her. "I'm not going to move your arm, just trying to secure it so when I lift you your arm stays as still as possible."

Pain etched her face as he stabilized the arm, but she didn't make a sound. When he was done, he leaned down and kissed her forehead. "Are you ready?"

She nodded.

He slipped his arms underneath her, trying his best not to move her arm any more than necessary. She moaned at the motion so he stopped. "What hurts?"

"Arm."

He continued to lift her. When he was standing, he asked, "You okay?"

She leaned her head against his shoulder. "I am now."

He hurried to the cabin as fast and with as much care as possible. The horses followed him. Once inside, he sat down on the old sofa, holding her close.

Cradling her broken arm with his left hand, he carefully took his right hand and reached into his coat pocket for his phone. She moaned. "Sorry, trying to be as gentle as I can."

"I know."

Hank picked up on the first ring.

"She's awake. We're in the cabin."

"We're almost there."

Hanging up, Shane looked into her deep blue eyes. "I was so afraid."

"I knew you would come." With her good arm, she reached up and touched his face. "I love you, Shane."

His heart exploded with joy. "I love you, too." He started to lower his lips to hers when the door burst open and her father and brothers rushed in. Ben immediately dropped down beside them. "How you doing, kiddo?"

"You're not a people doctor," she said, barely opening her eyes.

"I'm the best you got right now."

She grimaced when he touched her arm. "I'm in trouble then."

"Well, we know she's going to be alright. The smart mouth is alive and well," Ben teased. They all watched as Ben gently felt for broken bones. "She's okay to transport." He made a motion as if to take her from Shane.

"No, I have her."

Ben nodded. Hank held the door open, touching her face as they went by. She managed a smile. "I'm okay, Daddy."

Shane gently set her in the back seat. He wanted to go with her, but someone had to bring the horses back.

Jake came up behind him, reading his mind. "I'll get the horses back. You go with Cassidy."

"But Antony?"

"I'll ride Cleo, and we all know Antony will follow along."

Shane nodded. He couldn't say thanks. The words choked up inside him. Instead he climbed in beside her. She leaned her head on his shoulder.

Hank got behind the wheel. "You okay, girl?"

"Yes."

"If I go too fast or hit too many bumps, you let me know."

"I'm okay, Daddy."

"When we get to the house, the ambulance is already waiting."

"I don't..."

"Cassidy, you do," Ben said. "You don't have to be a doctor to know your arm is broken and you have a concussion. You most likely need stitches in your head."

Hank hit a bump and Cassidy moaned.

"Sorry, baby," he said.

Shane put his arm around her, holding her tight so the bumps wouldn't jar her so much. She looked up into his eyes. "You're my hero."

"Forever and always."

Chapter 25

Because she had lost consciousness for over half an hour, they kept her in the hospital an extra day. She had been home for two days now, but there was no sign of Shane. She had tried calling him to let him know she was home. Not that she needed to do that, she was told he never left the hospital until she was taken to a private room. She didn't understand why he wasn't coming around. There was no doubt he had heard what she said. He had said it back. So what was the problem?

It wasn't the blizzard keeping him away. He had a phone. She stood at the doors to the balcony in her room staring out toward him. *Where are you, Shane?* She picked up her phone and called him. No answer. She called Allison. "What's going on with Shane?"

"What do you mean?"

"I've tried calling him and he doesn't answer. I've left messages, texted him, and still no reply."

"Ahh. You don't like it when the shoe is on the other foot, do you?"

"That's not fair."

"Isn't it?"

Cassidy sat on her bed. "I told him I loved him."

"He thinks you just said that because of your concussion."

"Why would he believe that?"

"For the past eight months, you have made it quite clear you wanted nothing to do with him, outside the school or rodeo. And suddenly you hit your head and now you're back in love with him."

"I have always loved him."

"I know that," Allison said. "But you've done a very good job of convincing him that you didn't."

"How do I make this right?"

"I don't know." Allison paused. "I would tell you to talk to him, but we know how well that advice went over with you."

Cassidy heard Christmas music in the background. "What were you doing?"

"Wrapping presents and listening to music."

"Wrap up a Christmas miracle for me."

"I have five years of that request already sent above."

She disconnected and texted Shane: *Please forgive me. I love you.* She laid in bed staring at the ceiling waiting for the ding of a text that never came.

When the doctor had said Cassidy would be alright, he was just keeping her for observation, Shane left. No way could he look into her eyes and see the coolness return. He turned off his phone. Purposeful silence was better than waiting for a call that would never come. He knew because he had been waiting for one for five years.

He would savor the memory of the love in her eyes and the sound of her voice saying I love you until he had no choice but to deal with the realization it was all a mistake.

He grabbed his heavy coat and gloves, dropped his cell phone in his pocket, and went out to start the plow. The snow had finally ended, not that a couple feet of snow ever stopped Wyomingites from coming to a party. That night's Christmas Eve celebration was one of the biggest events of the year. The house would be full of family and good friends.

His heart constricted, knowing once again she would be so close and yet so far away. He glanced at the sky. *God, how do I fix this?*

"Turn on your phone."

Shane slammed on the brake of the plow. He had clearly heard the voice in his head. He pulled the phone from his pocket and turned it on. Within seconds, the *ding ding ding* of messages vibrated in his hand. The first thing he saw was her text from yesterday.

Please forgive me. I love you.

He quickly dialed Cassidy's number. No answer. He started to text back: *I love you too,* but stopped. No. Those were words needed to be spoken in person. Instead, he texted:

see you tonight

Rachel and Hank were the first to arrive as always. They had come early to help with whatever needed to be done. Disappointment filled Shane when Cassidy wasn't with them.

Rachel hugged him. "She'll be here later. Not much she can do with one arm in a sling."

"How's she getting here?"

"Jake is bringing her."

"I could go get her."

"No, Shane. Let her come to you."

He nodded. Isn't that what everyone had been saying all along? *Let her find her way back to you.* He took a deep breath. He had waited five years. What was another hour or two?

He appointed himself doorman, taking everyone's hats and coats as they entered, putting them on the bed in the guest bedroom. It was going on seven and still no Cassidy. Where were they?

He was putting coats in the guest room when he heard his father say, "There's the World Champion Bull Rider who breaks her arm falling off a horse."

By the time Shane got into the hallway, his father had whisked her away.

He heard her saying, "I'll never live this one down, will I?"

"What fun would that be?"

Shane stood watching her. As always, she took his breath away, but tonight more than usual. The light from the Christmas tree glistened off the rhinestones on her red dress. Her smile lit up the room when she turned and saw him. He rushed to her side.

"Sorry we're late." She looked down at her boots. "I had trouble getting ready." She looked at her brother. "And someone doesn't know how to put boots on another person."

Jake shrugged. "Who knew it would be so difficult?"

"You're here now, that's all that matters." He linked his arm in hers. "Can we talk?"

"I would like that."

He led her down the hall, into the sitting room. She looked around. A Christmas tree lit all in white was in the corner and a fire was burning in the fireplace. On the coffee table in front of the loveseat was a bouquet of roses. Two champagne glasses filled with a pink bubbly liquid were on either side of the roses. She looked up at him in surprise. "What's all this?"

He pointed to the roses. "For you." He winked. "The champagne is pink lemonade with a splash of 7-Up."

She giggled. "This is very romantic."

He led her to the loveseat. Careful to avoid the cast on her right arm, he sat to her left. Taking her free hand in his, he said, "Cassidy—"

She put her finger to his lips. "Let me go first." She gently touched his face. "I need you to know that my pushing you away had nothing to do with loving you. I never stopped, not for a minute."

He started to say something but Cassidy interrupted him again. "Miranda cornered me at the first rodeo the following season after it happened." Cassidy took Shane's hand in hers, rubbing her finger gently back and forth. "And she refused to let me leave until she explained what happened." Cassidy let out a deep sigh. "Yes, I still felt betrayed, but I forgave you."

"If you forgave me—"

A tear slipped from her eye. "That stupid kiss alone wasn't what utterly crushed my heart."

He wiped the tear from her face. "I did something else?"

"You didn't come after me." Her voice choked up. "You chose the rodeo over me." She looked away. "Proving to me that what I thought we had wasn't real. I could no longer trust you or my heart. It was all a lie."

"Oh, Cassidy," his voice filled with emotions. "You have to know I wanted to."

"But you didn't. For ten days, you stayed in Vegas. Each day that you didn't come was another nail in my heart."

He pulled her to him. "Don't you know I wanted to? But I couldn't, I was trapped there. I had Luke, Allison, and their horses with me. Luke was just barely nineteen, and neither he nor Allison could drive my big rig. Every second I was there, I was dying inside." He lifted her face so he could see into her eyes. "It was the first and only time I went to Vegas and won nothing. Jake was so mad at me. We came in last in Team Roping. If I could even manage to rope the calf, my time was too slow. We finished in last place. After the first few days, I pulled out of the other events. I couldn't focus. If I'd continued, one of those bulls would have killed me, because all I could think about was you. I kept calling, but you wouldn't pick up."

"I was so hurt. I couldn't." She squeezed his hand.

"Will you believe me when I say you are first place in my heart and always will be?"

She nodded her head. "These past eight months have shown me that. You placed my dream of being a World Champion over yours of being a three-time consecutive World Champion. And yet, seeing firsthand that you were putting me first, something inside me still refused to let you in."

"What changed?"

"I ran into Mr. Triplett last week and he said something that shook me to the core." She lowered her hand and started toying with the fringe of her white shawl. "He made me realize it wasn't that I *couldn't* trust you... it was that I *wouldn't.*"

Shane took her hand in his for a moment.

She looked down, then up into his eyes. Her own glistened with tears. "I have loved you for as long as I can remember. And I was willing to throw it away over one misunderstanding. It was more important to my stupid pride to punish you, instead of trusting you again."

She stood and went over to the Christmas tree. She found the ornament she was looking for, the glass manger. She gently touched it. "Mr. Triplett said something else. And to be honest, I never realized it until his words echocd in my head on the ride with Cleopatra."

Shane came up behind her, putting his hands around her waist, drawing her against him. "What was that?"

"He said there was no doubt in anybody's mind that our love was a gift from God."

He kissed her neck. "I believe that."

"I do, too." She turned around, leaning her head on his chest. "Oh, Shane, I've been so stupid. Don't you see, not only did I slam the door on you, I locked God out too? By not trusting you, I was saying God was wrong and couldn't be trusted." She took a step back, placing her hand against her chest. Tears flowed down her face. "For five years, I have felt this evilness wrapped around my heart. Right before the elk scared Cleo and me half to death, I asked God to forgive me. Shane, will you ever forgive me?"

He gently kissed her and said, "*Mon coeur*, without you, I have no heart. Of course, I forgive you." He grinned and winked at her. "Seems like we both have been idiots. But these two idiots," he said pointing from him to her, "love each other more than life itself. I love you, Cassidy, and nothing will ever again break us apart." He pulled her into his arms and gently swept her back. "I love you." When his lips touched hers, a volcano of joy erupted throughout his body, and he knew forever and always his heart was back where it belonged.

"I love you, Shane," she said in a breathless whisper.

He lifted her back up. With a quick kiss, he released her. Kneeling, he reached under the tree for a lone red velvet box. "I've been carrying this around for five years. It's time it found its way to where it belongs." Remaining on one knee, he flipped the lid open, took her hand in his then turned the box for her to see. The clusters of diamonds glistened like stars under the white Christmas lights. Cassidy threw her hand over her mouth.

"*Mon coeur*, will you marry me?"

She threw her arm around him, nearly knocking them both to the floor. "Yes, yes, yes." Tears of joy trickled down her cheeks.

He placed the ring on her finger and looked upward. "Thank you, God, for my Christmas miracle."

"Our Christmas miracle."

Spiritual Hero

Mr. Willis Triplett

In each of my books, one character is based on a real person who comes from a small group of unique people who have touched not only my heart but my spirit. I call these people my spiritual heroes.

These people carry the love of Jesus so completely, you cannot help but be drawn to them. When they entered my life, I was truly blessed, and though many of them are no longer here on earth, their presence in my life remains a driving force in how I live.

In *A Memory Like You*, that person is Mr. Willis Triplett. I must say that when I first met him I thought he was just an old fuddy-dud. Looking back, I really don't think he was as old as I remember, but when you are a young teen, anyone over thirty is ancient. Unfortunately for him, he had replaced our much loved and younger Sunday School teacher, and we were not happy. There was definitely a generation gap between him and our class and I'm ashamed to say I don't think we were that nice to him.

Fast forward a few years and my grandmother died on Christmas Eve. When most people would have been enjoying the holidays with family, Mr. Triplett made the hour drive to be with my family at the first viewing. I was so shocked to see him. I asked why he had come all that way. He said, "Your family needed me." That moment was the turning point in how I viewed Mr. Triplett.

My mother later struggled with health issues and every time she was in the hospital, Mr. Triplett once again made the hour-plus trip to visit her.

Then something happened in his family, something I felt surely would flip him out. Much to my surprise, he handled it with grace, love, and acceptance. By watching him I discovered how a man filled with the love of Jesus acts. Mr. Triplett became someone I not only admired, but the first man I can ever remember feeling respect for outside my family.

He was a man who carried Jesus not just to church, but everywhere he went. I was so blessed to have him in my life. Even now, writing this fills my heart with the joy of his memory and the lessons he taught me.

Mr. Triplett, you are truly my spiritual hero. I love you.

Other Books by this Author

"...page after page of inspiring words and photographs showing us how God uses nature to speak to us. A genuine treat for the eyes!"

~Loree Lough, best-selling author of 119 award-winning books

"The photographs and inspiring words of Vickie Fisher's HELLO GOD, ARE YOU THERE? filled my heart with joy and reminded me to look for the blessing of each day."

~Susan Meier, bestselling Harlequin author of A Father for Her Triplets

"...one of the strongest heroines, because she sticks to her moral code and religious beliefs in the face of her steaming hot love for Nick."

—*Connie C. Scharon, Amazon best-selling author of* Enchanted Lover

After three long months in Mexico, PSA's top security agent Nicholas McFadden doesn't want another assignment. Then he hears her name – Brittany Fitzpatrick. Now he knows he can't refuse.

Ten years ago she almost made him believe in love, until she lied and nearly got him killed. Now PSA wants him to protect her from the very man who almost murdered them both. Can he trust her? Or is this just another evil plot by Vincent Capri to finish the job?

"Flowers and pups, love and miracles... and robust faith that answers unasked questions and overshadows every fear."

—*Loree Lough, bestselling author of 119 award-winning novels, including reader favorites like* 50 Hours *and* A Man of Honor

He was never so happy as the day they met, now he's never been so scared to lose her.

Jeff and Michelle's lives had felt as perfect as their love for one another. A successful family business, wonderful children, and the hope of a long life together... until an inoperable brain tumor threatens to destroy the happily ever after they thought was guaranteed. Will faith and sacrifice be enough to save the woman he can't imagine life without?

About the Author

Vickie Fisher lives on nineteen tranquil acres in Westminster, Maryland. She works for Amtrak as a chief entitlement clerk. In her spare time, she enjoys spending time with her children, grandchildren, family and friends, who she believes are God's greatest gifts. When she isn't writing she is taking photographs of nature.

Contact the author at:

Vickiefisher.com
vickie.fisher@verizon.net